THE PET FINDERS CLUB

THE PET FINDERS CLUB

THE PET FINDERS CLUB

Runaway Rascal

BEN M. BAGLIO

Hodder
Children's
Books

A division of Hachette Children's Books

Special thanks to Lucy Courtenay

Text copyright © 2006 Working Partners Ltd
Illustration copyright © 2008 Cecilia Johansson

First published in the USA in 2006 by Scholastic Inc

First published in Great Britain in 2008
by Hodder Children's Books

The rights of Ben M Baglio and Cecilia Johansson to be
identified as the Author and Illustrator of the Work respectively
have been asserted by them in accordance with the
Copyright, Designs and Patents Act 1988

1

ISBN-13: 978 0 340 93138 7

Typeset in Weiss by Avon DataSet Ltd,
Bidford on Avon, Warwickshire

Printed in the UK by CPI Bookmarque, Croydon, CR0 4TD

The paper and board used in this paperback by Hodder Children's
Books are natural recyclable products made from wood grown in
sustainable forests. The manufacturing processes conform to the
environmental regulations of the country of origin.

Hodder Children's Books
a division of Hachette Children's Books
338 Euston Road, London NW1 3BH
An Hachette Livre UK Company

Chapter One

Andi Talbot frowned at her open suitcase. She was sure she'd only packed one jumper so far, and suddenly there were three.

She looked at the little tan-and-white terrier lying at the end of her bed. "Did you put these in here, Buddy?" she asked.

The terrier pricked up his ears before settling his head back on his paws. Andi reached over to rub his neck.

"Mum?" she called. "Did you put all these extra jumpers in my case?"

"It's only March, Andi," Judy Talbot said, coming into the room. "This is England, not Texas, remember? You'll need those jumpers when you're staying at the Saunderses'. The forecast is wet and cold this week."

Andi sighed. She preferred the hot Texas weather, where she and her mum used to live. A wet forecast for the spring half-term holiday was one of the downsides of moving to England.

"Oh, don't forget to pack enough socks," her mum added, "or you might have to borrow a pair of Tristan's."

"*Euw*." Andi shuddered.

"You are OK about me going to this conference, aren't you?" Judy Talbot said anxiously. "It's only for a week."

"Stop worrying, Mum," Andi said, heading for the bathroom to collect her toothbrush. "We'll have a great time."

Although she was going to miss her mum, Andi was really looking forward to staying with Tristan Saunders. He and Natalie Lewis were her two best friends in Aldcliffe, a suburb of Lancaster. They'd set up the Pet Finders Club when Andi had first moved here, after she'd lost Buddy for a few days following her move to England.

"I know you might have preferred to stay with Natalie, but it just wasn't possible this week," her mum continued as Andi returned with her toothbrush. "They've got their hands full with the party, not to mention their houseguest. Miranda arrived last night, didn't she?"

"Melissa," Andi corrected, tucking her toothbrush into her suitcase.

"Pretty name," said Mrs Talbot. "Is Natalie getting on OK with her? I understood from Mrs Peterson that she's doing a favour for Melissa's mum by having her to stay."

Natalie hadn't sounded that impressed with her guest when Andi had spoken to her the night before. But Andi didn't want to sound unkind. "I think they're . . . a bit different," she said.

"Ah well," Mrs Talbot said diplomatically. "At least they've got the party to think about."

Natalie's stepdad would be forty at the end of the week and, according to Natalie, her mum was planning the party of the century. She had shared every detail of the plans with Andi: the jazz band with their white jackets and gold bow ties, the

Thai-style nibbles, Natalie's pale-blue beaded outfit and her mum's red satin ball-gown.

Just before she took her case downstairs, Andi managed to sneak out one of the jumpers and replace it with her comfiest hoodie. She added a couple more books and tossed in an extra CD. Then she closed the case and carried it down with Buddy close at her heels.

It was only a five-minute drive to the Saunderses' house, where Tristan, his parents and his brother, Dean, were waiting for them. After Andi had said goodbye to her mum (and promised to wear a jumper at least once that week) the whole family helped to carry Andi's bags inside.

"It's really kind of you to have me and Bud, Mrs Saunders," Andi said gratefully. "Are you sure Lucy's going to be OK having Buddy around?"

Mrs Saunders smiled. "Lucy can stick up for herself," she said. "If Buddy puts a foot wrong, Lucy'll put him in his place."

Andi put Buddy in the back garden, where he started happily sniffing his way round the flowerbeds. The sky was beginning to look grey and threatening, and Andi knew they'd have rain before long.

"Dean's doing pizza for lunch, but that won't be for ages yet," Tristan explained. "Would you like to have a go at my new PC game? I'm already pretty good at it," he added, "so don't worry if you don't win – like, ever!"

"Sounds great," Andi told him, pulling a face.

"I think Andi might prefer to unpack first," Mrs Saunders suggested. "She's here all week, Tristan. The game can wait!"

"This is where you'll be staying," Mr Saunders announced, leading the way upstairs and opening a door across the landing from Tristan's room.

"I'm sorry we can't stay and help you settle in," Mrs Saunders apologized. "There's a new housing estate being built on the east side of Aldcliffe that we've got to look at this morning. Enjoy your pizza!"

Tristan's parents ran an estate agent's and when they weren't at home, Tristan's older brother, Dean, took charge. He was an excellent cook, if a little experimental. Andi wondered nervously what the pizza toppings would be.

After Tristan's parents had left, Andi looked round for Tristan's cat. "Where's Lucy?"

"On a beautiful morning like this?" Tristan said, heading into the kitchen. Outside, the sky was looking increasingly dark and ominous. "Where any self-respecting cat would be: on my bed. Listen, Andi, I don't think Luce is looking forward to seeing Buddy," he warned. "She's been sharpening her claws ever since I told her you and Bud were coming to stay."

"Your mum thinks they'll be fine," said Andi. "Buddy likes cats."

"Of course he does," Tristan said, only half joking. "Between two slices of bread."

He was very protective of his beautiful silver tabby, Lucy, who had gone missing for several months before Andi and the Pet Finders Club had tracked her down.

"Buddy's only chased Lucy once before," Andi pointed out.

Tristan looked unconvinced. "Lucy sleeps in the

kitchen overnight," he said. "I thought we could put Buddy in the utility room so we can shut the door."

"Relax," Andi told him. "Bud's got loads of new places to sniff and a new garden to run around in. The last thing on his mind will be chasing Lucy." She wasn't totally convinced that this was true, but she didn't want to worry Tristan. Opening the back door, she called, "Buddy! Here, boy!"

Buddy raced inside and made straight for Lucy's cat bed, which was tucked into a cosy corner of the kitchen. He sniffed it with interest and gave a little yip. On cue, Lucy came into the kitchen, her soft paws making no noise on the tiled floor. Tristan went to scoop her up, but Andi laid her hand on his arm.

"Let's see what happens," she suggested.

Lucy stopped when she saw Buddy and looked as though she was going to take a step back. Then she hissed. Buddy cocked his head and pricked up his ears. *Please don't chase her*, Andi prayed, ready to grab the terrier by the scruff of the neck if he made a move.

After staring at each other for a couple of

seconds, Lucy hissed again. Then she padded closer and sniffed at Buddy's nose. Buddy tried to lick her, but Lucy's paw shot out and cuffed him round the ear. Her claws weren't out, but Buddy looked quite shocked! He promptly lay down and rolled on to his back, as if he wanted to make friends. Lucy gave him a withering look from her beautiful blue eyes, then stalked past him and had a drink from her water bowl.

"Poor old Buddy," Andi said. "But don't worry, I'm sure she'll get used to you." Beside her, Tristan looked very relieved.

The doorbell shrilled and Tristan went to open the door, with Andi and Buddy following close behind. Natalie, her black Labrador, Jet, and a girl Andi had never seen before stood on the porch. Above their heads, there was a rumble of thunder and rain began pattering on the slate roof of the porch. Andi bent down and picked up Buddy, remembering that it was a storm that had frightened him into running away when they first moved to Aldcliffe.

"Jet is totally mad today," Natalie said, as her

excitable dog tried to jump up at everyone in the porch. "This is Melissa," she added, waving her hand at the girl standing next to her. "Melissa, this is Andi and Tristan, and Andi's dog, Buddy. My mum and Melissa's mum have been friends for years. Thanks for the invitation to lunch, by the way. Pizza's my favourite."

When Natalie stopped to breathe, Melissa smiled shyly. She had blonde hair cut in a feathery style that framed her small heart-shaped face, and she was wearing jeans and a blue jacket. The way she tilted her head to one side reminded Andi of a little bird.

"Oh, I almost forgot!" Natalie squeaked, delving into her bag and pulling out two long cream envelopes. "Here's your invitation to the party, Tris, and yours too, Andi. Don't they look great?"

Tristan tore open his envelope. "You are invited to a birthday celebration," he read aloud from the neat rectangle of thick creamy card. Overhearing, Dean came out of the kitchen to find out about the invitation, and introduced himself to Melissa with a smile.

"I wanted Mum to send us one," Natalie said earnestly, "but she said no."

"You wanted an invitation to your own party?" Tristan said in surprise.

"It's so exciting when you get invitations in the post," Natalie explained. "It's better than all the boring stuff that usually comes. No one ever sends me anything."

"Except Neil," Melissa piped up. "Ouch! Why did you step on my toe, Natalie?"

Natalie had gone bright pink. Tristan and Andi turned and looked at her questioningly.

"Neil?" Andi echoed. "Would that be Neil O'Connor, from Riverside Stables? What's he been sending you?"

Neil O'Connor's mum ran a riding stable outside Aldcliffe, where Andi and Natalie had been taking Western-style lessons.

Natalie tossed her hair. "It was just a postcard," she said. "He's staying with his cousins in York for a few days. It doesn't mean anything."

Tristan raised his eyebrows so high, they nearly disappeared into his red hair. "A postcard from your boyfriend? It sounds to me as though it means a lot."

"He's not my boyfriend!"

"You said he was this morning," Melissa said, looking puzzled.

"I did *not*," Natalie said. "You must have heard me wrong." Looking flustered, she bent down to take off Jet's lead. Jet promptly leapt away from her and chased Buddy into the kitchen.

"Sorry I had to bring Melissa along," Natalie whispered to Andi as they ran into the kitchen after the two dogs. "Mum sprung her on me this week. Her parents have gone to Hong Kong, but Melissa didn't want to go, so her mum thought it would be fun for her to spend the holidays in Aldcliffe. I can't think why Melissa agreed to it. I mean, who would pick Aldcliffe over Hong Kong?"

Andi glanced back at the hall, where Tristan and Dean were talking to Melissa. She was laughing at something Tristan had said. "She seems nice," Andi said.

"She's OK." Natalie shrugged. "We don't know each other very well. I mean, we meet a couple of times a year when our mums get together, but that's all."

There was a volley of barking and claw-scrabbling from the utility room, followed by a spitting noise. Jet yelped. Moments later, a Lucy-shaped blur streaked past Andi and Natalie and straight up the stairs.

"It sounds as though Lucy showed Jet who's boss," Andi joked as they made their way back into the hall. Buddy and Jet had flopped down on the tiled floor with their tongues hanging out, so they left them in the kitchen. "She's got her paws full today keeping the dogs in their place."

"Lunch will be ready in about an hour," Dean said, heading past in the other direction.

"Let's go into the living room," Tristan suggested. "The dogs can come in there with us."

"It'll be a pets' party," Andi grinned.

"That would be my perfect party," Melissa said enthusiastically.

Andi was pleased. It sounded as though she and Melissa had something in common. "Have you got any pets, Melissa?"

"A dwarf rabbit," she replied, her face lighting up. "Her name's Rascal."

"And is she?" Tristan asked. "A rascal, I mean?"

"She's already tried to eat my new slippers," Natalie grumbled, joining Andi on the squashy settee beneath the window.

"You've brought Rascal to Aldcliffe?" Andi asked Melissa in surprise.

Melissa nodded. "Rascal's very highly strung, and she gets unhappy without me," she said. "We tried a petsitter once, but Rascal got really nervous. It took ages to get her back into her usual routine. So I thought I'd bring her with me. Mum and Dad took a bit of persuading, but Natalie's parents were really kind and said it would be OK. It's only half an hour's drive from home, and she sat on my lap in her pet-carrier the whole time. She was really good."

"And now she's running round my bedroom eating my stuff," Natalie sighed.

"She didn't eat your slippers," Melissa said. "She just sniffed them a bit."

"She sniffed them with her *teeth*," Natalie

corrected her. When Melissa looked upset, she added quickly, "But she is cute."

"She's the softest thing you've ever felt," Melissa said dreamily. "Honestly, sometimes I stroke her and it's like I can hardly even feel her fur. She's an indoor rabbit, so she's house-trained and everything. She's the best pet in the world."

Andi thought of the comforting roughness of Buddy's coat. It sounded as though having a rabbit would be totally different. "I'd love to meet Rascal," she said.

She was about to ask if they could come and see Rascal some time that week when her mobile phone started ringing. Andi fished it out of her pocket. "Hello?"

Her mum's voice crackled into her ear. "I'm at the airport, darling," she said. "I just thought I'd check that you're settling in OK. Have you offered to help Mrs Saunders with dinner tonight, as we discussed?"

"I haven't had a chance yet," Andi said, shifting the mobile phone to her other ear and glancing apologetically at the others.

"Well, don't forget," Mrs Talbot continued. "It's hard work having people to stay. Is your room nice?"

"Mum, can we talk about this later?"

"Oh, OK," her mum said. "Just remember—"

"Bye, Mum," Andi said firmly, and hung up. She turned back to Melissa. "I was going to ask if we could come round and see Rascal—"

Her phone started ringing again. Impatiently, Andi clicked it on. "Mum, I really can't talk now," she began.

"Uh, hello?" said a boy's voice. He sounded close to tears. "Is that the Pet Finders Club?"

Andi slithered to the edge of the sofa, instantly alert. "Yes?"

"I saw your poster on a telegraph pole near my house," said the boy. "My name's Will Jacobs. It's about my cat, Tiger. He's gone missing. Please say you'll find him. *Please!*"

Chapter Two

Andi covered the mouthpiece of the phone with her hand and hissed, "Tris, Nat, we've got a missing cat called Tiger. Get me some paper, quick!"

Tristan produced a pad of paper from a table at the side of the room, while Natalie took a pen out of her bag.

Andi tucked the phone more securely under her chin. "What's your address, Will?" She scribbled it down. "We'll be there in ten minutes," she promised, and hung up.

Melissa looked confused. "What was all that about? Where's 'there'?"

"25 Oakley Avenue," Andi read. "That's just round the corner."

Tristan had fetched his rucksack from the hall and was peering inside.

"Notebook?" Natalie said. "Pencil? Plastic wallet for photographs?"

"Yep, yep and yep," Tristan said, flipping the rucksack closed again.

"What's this about a missing cat? Why are we going to Oakley Avenue?" Melissa asked, following Andi and the others as they shut the dogs in the utility room and started putting on their coats.

"It's our Pet Finders Club," Natalie explained. "I told you about it, remember? That phone call was from a boy who's lost his cat, so we're going over to ask him questions that might help find it: when it went missing, what it looks like – stuff like that."

"But it's lunch in an hour," Melissa pointed out. "Can't it wait?"

Tristan stopped in his tracks. "Good point. Hey, Deano!" he called through the kitchen door. "We've got a PFC emergency. Melissa wondered if lunch could wait?"

"I didn't mean lunch," Melissa began.

18

Dean appeared at the kitchen door. "No problem," he said, drying his hands on his black-and-white checked apron. "See you about two."

"Two o'clock?" Melissa said in dismay. "But that means we won't be back at your house until after three, Natalie. I've got to feed Rascal at two o'clock."

"The Pet Finders Club always comes first with us, Melissa," Andi explained gently. "We drop whatever we're doing and start looking for the missing pet. Every minute is vital."

"It might not take much time," Tristan added. "We could still be back for pizza and get to Nat's place in time to feed Rascal."

Melissa looked unconvinced.

"Let's see how it goes," Natalie said. "If we have to leave early to feed Rascal, we will. Tristan and Andi can come over this afternoon to tell me anything I missed, and play with Rascal. If that's OK?"

"That would be great," Melissa said, looking a little happier. She took down her coat from the peg in the hall, then gasped as she looked out of

19

the window. Sheets of rain were hammering down. "It's really wet out there," she said. "Do we *have* to go out?"

"It's only a shower," Natalie said, raising her voice over the furious drumming on the windows. "You're going to love pet-finding, Melissa. It's all part of the Aldcliffe experience!"

Tristan found three umbrellas in the porch and they set out like a trio of brightly-coloured mushrooms. Melissa was wearing new converse trainers, but she stepped round the worst puddles and didn't complain. Andi tucked her hand into the crook of her elbow to share the umbrella. When she gave Melissa a grin, she was relieved to see Melissa grin back.

The Jacobses' house was set a little way back from the road. There were three steps up to the front door and a freshly-painted white wooden porch, where Will Jacobs was waiting for them. He was an anxious-looking boy of about twelve, with a thin face and very dark brown eyes.

"Thanks for coming," he said.

"No problem," Andi replied as they shook

out their umbrellas and stood them neatly in the porch. "I'm Andi, and this is Tristan, Natalie and Melissa."

Will hung up their coats and led them into a large, airy kitchen, where they all sat round a dark wooden table.

Tristan pulled out his notebook and opened it at a fresh page. "OK, Will. What can you tell us?"

"Where should I start?" Will asked anxiously.

"Tell us exactly when Tiger went missing," Andi suggested.

"He didn't come home two nights ago," Will said. "That was a bit unusual, but Tiger's an independent cat. We looked all round the area yesterday, but we didn't want to raise the alarm in case he came back on his own. When he didn't come back last night either, Mum told me to phone you."

"Is your mum in?" Andi asked.

Will shook his head. "She had to go out. My dad's working upstairs."

"Can you tell us what Tiger looks like?" Natalie prompted.

Will clasped his hands round his knees. "He's a fat tabby cat with gorgeous gold and chocolate stripes, and a white tummy."

"Has he got a collar?" Andi said.

Will shook his head. "We tried to get him to wear one, but Tiger hated it and used to pull it off."

Tristan made a note.

"What's he like?" Natalie asked. "I mean, character-wise?"

"He's really affectionate . . ." Will stopped, and started picking at a frayed patch on his jeans. Andi noticed that his eyes looked a little wet. He cleared his throat and started again. "He's really affectionate and sociable, although he loves hunting outside on his own, too. Like I said, he's pretty independent, although he always comes back at night."

"You say he's been gone for two days?" Andi checked. Will nodded. "Is it unusual for him to miss his meals?"

Will shook his head. "Not really. He's picky with his food and doesn't always eat everything in his bowl, even though he's not exactly underweight. Actually, he's pretty heavy. I can't hold him for long without my arms starting to ache. His favourite food's sardines."

Tristan smiled at him. "My cat Lucy loves anchovies," he said. "She went missing too, you know. She was gone for six months, but we found her in the end. It's really worth staying positive."

Will gave a watery smile. "Thanks," he said. "I'll try."

Melissa, who was sitting on the arm of the couch, suddenly leant forward. "Is Tiger a playful cat?" she asked shyly. "My rabbit, Rascal, loves her toys." Andi gave her an encouraging smile.

Will nodded. "We've got a rubber mouse on elastic that he chases all over the place." He fished under the sofa and brought out the mouse, stretching it until it twanged back and whacked into the sofa's leg. "He's got loads of energy and always pesters me to play with him. Oh, and he's got this habit of leaping out of bushes and fussing round people's ankles. It's really funny."

"We'll start looking for him straight away,"

Tristan said, snapping his notebook shut. "You've looked in the house already, have you?"

Will nodded. "But I suppose it wouldn't do any harm to look again. Especially since you four are professionals."

The word "professional" made Andi feel very proud. "We'll quarter the inside of the house first," she suggested, with a nod from the others.

The Pet Finders slipped into their practised house-searching routine, with Melissa doing her best to keep up. Andi and Tristan started upstairs, while Natalie and Melissa helped Will downstairs. They opened cupboards, pulled back furniture, looked under beds. They pulled out all the curtains in case Tiger was hidden among the folds. They even looked underneath the bath, when Tristan found a handle which removed the front panel.

"Remember when we found a cat behind a bath panel?" he said to Andi as he carefully put the panel back. "It's always worth checking the weirdest places."

But there was no sign of Tiger anywhere.

Andi and Tristan trooped down the stairs.

Natalie, Melissa and Will were waiting anxiously at the bottom.

"No luck," Andi sighed.

"Nor us," Will said gloomily. "I'm not surprised. Tiger's an outdoor cat, mainly. He only comes in to play and sleep."

"What happens next?" Melissa asked Natalie.

"We'll check the garden; ask the neighbours if they've seen anything; borrow a photo of the missing pet, make posters and flyers and put them up around here; widen our search if we have to, report the missing pet to the local animal shelter and perhaps the police," Natalie reeled off.

"You do all that?" Melissa gasped. Natalie nodded. Andi realized it did sound like a lot, although sometimes it felt as if there was never enough they could do to find the missing animal.

She glanced out of the window. The rain had eased off and the sun was shining weakly on the garden. "Next thing we'll do is search outside," she said. "We'll ask the neighbours if we can look in their gardens too."

"We'll find Tiger for you," Melissa said to Will as

26

they trooped outside. "We'll find him up a tree, I expect. Rascal, my rabbit, goes missing all the time. I always totally panic and then I find her five minutes later."

Finding pets wasn't usually that easy, Andi knew. But Will looked happier at Melissa's confident words and Andi didn't want to spoil the mood. Crossing her fingers and hoping Melissa was right, she turned her attention to the search.

They picked their way between the shrubs, peered up trees, and poked and prodded the fence for any loose panels. Tristan hunted through the Jacobses' shed, and Natalie and Melissa checked the garage.

Underneath a prickly shrub at the side of the house, Natalie found a clump of brownish-grey fur. "It's a clue!"

Andi took the piece of fluff and held it up to get a better look at it. "I don't think it looks very tabby," she said doubtfully. "Will, what do you think?"

Will looked carefully at it. "Tiger's more golden than that, but he's got grey fur in his undercoat," he said. "You can see it sometimes when you part his fur right down to the skin."

"Can I see?" Melissa took the fur and rubbed it between her fingers. She frowned. "Sorry, but this is rabbit fur," she said, passing it to Tristan.

Andi was impressed. "How do you know?" she asked, taking the fluff from Tristan and rolling it between her fingers, the way she'd seen Melissa do.

"It's much finer than cat fur," Melissa said. "You can hardly feel the fibres when you rub it like this, see? Even really soft cats have thicker fibres in their coats than rabbits do. Throw it away, Andi. It's useless." She suddenly looked upset.

"Don't worry, Melissa," Tristan said. "That was amazing, the way you worked out that clue. You're part of the pet-finding team already!"

Melissa shrugged. "But we haven't found Tiger, have we?"

"It's very rare to find pets just by searching someone's house and garden," Andi reminded everyone.

"But it would have been nice, just this once," Natalie sighed.

28

"Look at it this way. It's probably a good thing that we haven't found Tiger too close to home," Andi said.

Melissa looked baffled. "Is it?"

"If you find a cat close to home but not *at* home, it's often because they're injured and can't physically make it those last few gardens," Tristan said carefully.

Injured – or worse, Andi felt like adding. She'd once looked for an old hunting dog in Arizona who had found a quiet space under a bush to die. It had been her most upsetting case.

Will looked as though he was on the verge of tears.

"Have you tried putting food outside Tiger's cat-flap?" Tristan hastily changed the subject. "He might come back, but he may be too scared to come inside. When cats go missing, it's often because they've been traumatized by something, and that makes them frightened of everything, even their home."

"I'll give it a try tonight," Will promised.

"You said Tiger was a bit overweight, didn't you?"

Natalie recalled. "That means he won't be too badly affected by a few days without food, and the layers of fat should keep him warm at night."

"And he's got plenty of water," Melissa pointed out, dabbling the tip of her rather soggy trainer in a nearby puddle.

Natalie hesitated, trying to phrase a delicate question. "Is it possible that Tiger's been adopted by someone else?" She glanced at Tristan. "It happened to Lucy, Tris. We should consider it."

"It's too soon," Andi decided. "Tiger's only been gone a couple of days. If he's still missing a week from now, perhaps we should think again."

"Tiger wouldn't forget me just like that," Will said uncertainly, "would he?"

There was an awkward pause. Melissa checked her watch. "Listen," she said, "I've got to go and feed Rascal. She gets grumpy if her food's late. Sorry, Will. I really thought we'd find Tiger for you today." She looked genuinely sad.

"We'll have to miss Dean's pizza," Natalie said.

"We'll come over straight after lunch," Andi promised. "We can bring Jet over, to save you collecting him from Tris's house first." Melissa and Natalie headed off, sharing the biggest umbrella between them.

"We should make a poster of Tiger," Andi said. "Have you got a photo we can use, Will?"

"Tiger's a bit camera-shy," Will said, "but I'll see what I can find. Wait here."

He disappeared for a few minutes. When he came back, he was holding three photographs. "Sorry they aren't that good," he apologized.

One of the pictures showed a glimpse of Tiger's tabby tail as the cat fled from the camera. Another was a blurry action shot as Tiger jumped up at something which looked like the mouse on elastic. The third picture was quite small, but it did show the whole of Tiger, not just a bit of him.

Andi tucked it inside one of the plastic wallets in Tristan's rucksack. "We'll bring it back as soon as we've made the posters," she promised. "Once we've put them up, we'll talk to the neighbours and widen our search if we have to. Stay positive, Will. We're only just getting started."

They all turned at the sound of someone coming

down the stairs. A tall, thin man with the same dark-brown eyes as Will appeared.

"Hello, Dad," Will said. "You're finished early."

"The quote didn't take as long as I thought it would," Mr Jacobs explained. "Modern houses aren't nearly as much hassle as the old ones when it comes to fitting air-conditioning. Hello," he said to Andi and Tristan. "Friends of Will's, are you?"

Will introduced them and explained about the Pet Finders Club.

"You've got to be a Saunders with that red hair," Mr Jacobs said to Tristan with a friendly smile. "You're the image of your dad. I've fitted air-conditioners on a couple of projects for your parents in the past. It's great that you're going to help us find Tiger. Listen, have you had lunch yet? You're welcome to stay."

"Thanks, Mr Jacobs, but my brother's expecting us home for pizza," Tristan explained.

Mr Jacobs nodded. "Another time, then."

Trying not to shiver too much in the damp air coming from the open front door, Andi told Will, "We'll make posters and flyers as soon as we can.

32

Then we'll be back in touch. And remember —"

"Stay positive," Will said with a determined nod.

After waving goodbye, Andi followed Tristan down the Jacobses' path. Her trainers squelched, still wet from their earlier walk. Andi reflected that it was tough to stay positive when there was water seeping between your toes.

Chapter Three

Dean's pizza toppings were creative, to say the least.

"I liked the sausage and jam combination," Tristan said as they headed for Natalie's house with the dogs trotting at their heels.

"You would," Andi said with a shudder. Even Buddy had turned his head away when she'd offered him her crust, which had a smear of jam clinging to it.

They walked up the path towards the wide steps and fluted columns of Natalie's house. As always, the front garden looked immaculate. Even the puddles looked perfectly round and shiny.

They took off their coats and shoes, and put Buddy and Jet in the small room by the front door to dry off.

"It's so handy, having this room just here," Andi said, as she finished towelling Buddy's feet. Buddy padded over to Jet's roomy basket and collapsed next to Jet with a sigh.

"Trust Natalie to have a dedicated dog room," Tristan agreed. "She told me it used to be the utility room, but her mum got tired of taking the washing up and down the stairs all the time, so they had a new utility room fitted upstairs. This place had a heater and was just the right size for a dog, so Nat started using it for Jet."

"You're keeping the dogs in there, aren't you?" Melissa hurried down the stairs as Andi and Tristan emerged from the dog room. "Rascal would be petrified if she saw them. Even if she *smelt* them she'd get scared."

Natalie came down the stairs more slowly. Catching Andi's eye, she pulled a face. She clearly thought Melissa was a bit over-protective of her rabbit.

"Hello," Natalie said out loud. "Did you get a picture of Tiger?"

They walked together into the kitchen, where

Natalie's mum was talking to Maria, the Peterson's housekeeper. Maria was looking angry.

"Ah, Melissa," Mrs Peterson said, looking round. "Did you use the bag of radicchio from the crisper-drawer for Rascal's lunch?"

Melissa looked guilty. "Um," she said. "I suppose I did."

Maria muttered something in Spanish and vigorously began scrubbing the saucepans in the sink.

Mrs Peterson looked flustered. "That was for *us* to eat," she said. "Radicchio is a bit too expensive for a rabbit!"

"I used up Rascal's own bag of lettuce and she was still hungry," Melissa said apologetically. "I'm really sorry."

She slowly unzipped the front of her jumper. A single, telltale sprig of radicchio popped out, followed by a little white nose, and finally the head of a small, pale-grey rabbit.

"You must be Rascal," Andi said with delight. "Melissa, she's gorgeous!"

"I know," Melissa said, smiling affectionately at the rabbit.

Rascal shook her head, making her ears flap. Wriggling halfway out of Melissa's jumper, she woffled her nose at the housekeeper.

Natalie laughed. "She's trying to tell Maria she's sorry, look!"

Maria's frown disappeared and she smiled as she came over to stroke Rascal's fur. No one could stay cross with such an adorable little creature.

Melissa cuddled Rascal under her chin. "Let's take you upstairs out of trouble," she said.

All the rabbits Andi knew lived outside in hutches, with wire-mesh runs. An indoor rabbit was a completely new idea. "Has Rascal got a cage?" she asked, as they followed Melissa up the stairs.

"She's got a mansion at home," Melissa explained.

"What, with a pool and everything?" Tristan gasped.

Andi pictured Rascal on a sun lounger with a fruit cocktail in one paw.

Melissa laughed. "No! It's lots of wire cages stacked on top of each other. She loves climbing round in it. But when I'm in, she mostly hops round the house."

Natalie pushed open the door to the games room. "Rascal stays in here since she ate my slippers."

"She did *not* eat your slippers!" Melissa insisted.

On the floor in the games room, near the snooker table, was a cage lined with curly wood shavings and with a nest of straw in one corner; beside the cage, a crock of water and a bowl of food pellets stood on a large plastic mat, and next to them was a litter tray. A couple of long cardboard tubes lay on the rug further off. The room looked pretty well-equipped for a rabbit holiday!

"We've barricaded off all the little spaces Rascal can fit into, so we don't lose her under or behind the furniture," Melissa explained. "She's got the run of the whole room, see?" She put Rascal down beside one of the tubes. The little rabbit sniffed at the tube opening, then shot through and out the other side.

"That's really cute!" Andi said as Rascal hopped round and ran through the tube again, this time in the opposite direction.

"That's nothing," Melissa said proudly. "Wait till

you see what Nat and I put together for her last night!"

Natalie started looking more enthusiastic and helped Melissa set up a collection of boxes, hoops and tubes in the middle of the floor. The finishing touch was a scaled-down seesaw made out of a book and an empty shampoo bottle. Once these were laid out, the games room resembled a miniature show-jumping arena.

"On the count of three . . ." Melissa said, setting Rascal down at one end of the course.

"Three!" the others shouted.

Rascal zoomed over the book seesaw and shot through the tubes, then hopped over the boxes and through the hoops. Every so often she gave an energetic little sideways kick, for what looked like the sheer fun of it. Andi thought it was one of the cutest things she'd ever seen!

Suddenly, two sets of paws charged up the stairs: one large, one small. Next moment, the door to the games room was shoved open – and Jet and Buddy tumbled in, barking joyfully.

"Rascal!" Melissa gasped, making a dash for her

pet. But the little rabbit took one look at the dogs and fled across the room. Within seconds, she had completely disappeared.

Natalie threw herself on Jet and managed to get hold of his collar, while Andi grabbed Buddy. They dragged the protesting dogs outside and shut the door, where they started scrabbling and whining to be let in again.

"Melissa, I'm really sorry," Nat panted. "I looked in on Jet before we came upstairs, and I thought I'd shut the door. Where's Rascal?"

"I don't know!" Melissa wailed. "She's disappeared! First Tiger, now Rascal. I must be bad luck or something!"

Natalie kept apologizing, but Melissa was too upset to listen. Andi and Tristan started looking for the little rabbit, upending the cardboard tubes and peering behind the curtains.

"She can't have got behind the furniture," Natalie said, perplexed. "We blocked everything off, I'm sure we did."

They all stared round the apparently rabbitless room.

"Can rabbits teleport?" Tristan asked.

Suddenly Melissa made a dive toward Rascal's cage. "Look!" she said with delight. "She's put herself to bed!" Triumphantly, she burrowed her hand into the nest of straw and gently pulled the little rabbit out. Rascal was trembling all the way from her ears to her powder-puff tail, but as Melissa stroked her and murmured soothingly to her she began to calm down.

"Isn't she clever?" Melissa marvelled. "She knew she'd be safe in her cage!"

"We should have looked there first," Andi groaned, staring at the mess they'd made. "Now we'll have to tidy everything up again."

"This is all my fault, Melissa," Natalie said. She looked really upset with herself. "Is Rascal OK?"

"She's fine," said Melissa.

Tristan reached over and stroked Rascal's downy head with one finger. "Poor little thing," he said. "She's still shaking." He looked at Natalie. "I think you should keep Jet downstairs while Rascal's staying here. What if he got into the games room again? Rascal could get hurt."

Melissa beamed at Tristan. "Thanks," she said. "It's great to have someone who understands."

Tristan went red. "We've already got one lost pet to deal with," he said. "We don't want another one."

Andi and Natalie left the room to take the dogs back downstairs.

Natalie hunkered down to give Jet a cuddle. "You wouldn't do that again, would you?" she said, fondling his velvety black ears. "I don't really have to shut you downstairs." She sounded as though she was trying to convince herself.

Andi picked up Buddy, who wriggled and tried to lick her face. "Dogs can't help being bigger than rabbits," she said sympathetically to Natalie. "It really would be better to keep Jet downstairs."

"OK," Natalie said reluctantly. "I'll put him back in the dog room. Come on, Jet. Let's go." She stood up and hooked her fingers under Jet's collar to lead him down the stairs. Andi followed her with Buddy tucked tightly under her arm.

Down in the dog room, Natalie rubbed Jet's tummy, making him squirm with delight. "It seems a bit unfair, shutting him in here," she sighed as Andi put Buddy down. "Melissa and Rascal are taking over the whole house."

"It won't be for long," Andi reminded her. "Jet'll be fine."

She went over to tickle Jet's ears. When she turned back to Buddy, the little terrier had vanished.

Andi's first frantic thought was that Buddy had run upstairs again. But she found him in the kitchen, sitting hopefully at Maria's feet as the housekeeper chopped pieces of meat for a casserole.

"First the radicchio, now the casserole," Andi scolded, picking Buddy up. "If it was down to the animals in this house, Nat's family wouldn't have anything to eat!"

Andi woke up the following day with Buddy enthusiastically licking her face. She squinted up at the unfamiliar ceiling for a moment before she remembered where she was. She and Tristan had stayed up late the previous night to make a poster about Tiger. The photo Will had given them wasn't particularly good, but the poster was bright and colourful and was sure to get people's attention.

Twitching back the curtains, Andi saw it was another wet, cold day. Perhaps all those jumpers her mum had packed would come in useful after all. Downstairs, Mr Saunders was eating toast and looking through the newspaper, while opposite, Mrs Saunders was eating cereal and putting on her earrings at the same time.

"Morning!" she called as Tristan and Andi came into the kitchen.

"Pet-finding again?" Mr Saunders studied the sheaf of posters that Andi had put on the breakfast bar. "Nice poster. Shame about the photo. It's rather small."

"I know," Andi said. "I enlarged it as much as I could but you can hardly see Tiger at all."

"I'll take a poster and a handful of flyers for the office," Mrs Saunders offered, scooping them up and putting them into her briefcase. "Are you meeting Natalie today?"

"Later probably. Natalie and her friend Melissa are going shopping for party outfits this morning,"

Andi explained, pouring some orange juice. Natalie had rung the previous night to say that she'd changed her mind about her blue beaded dress and needed to find something else. Melissa loved shopping too, so they were going together. Andi felt a tiny bit relieved that Natalie didn't want her to go shopping with them. She knew she wouldn't be able to concentrate on party outfits while Tiger was still missing.

"We'll be back early tonight," Mrs Saunders said. She winked. "Hopefully I'll be able to save you from one of Dean's unusual culinary efforts."

After breakfast, Andi and Tristan snapped on Buddy's lead and stepped out into the grey morning, clutching a bundle of posters and flyers each. Soon half the trees between Tristan's house and Will's were adorned with posters, and every letterbox had had a flyer pushed through.

"Hello!" Will came hurrying down the steps of his house towards them. He looked tired, as though he hadn't slept much. "I've been looking out for you. Can I see Tiger's poster?"

Andi showed it to him. "We've put up almost half of them already."

"The photo I gave you has turned out really blurry," Will said, looking worried.

"But the rest of the poster's nice and bright," Andi said encouragingly. "People will stop and read them, don't worry. Come on, let's post a few more of these and then we'll start talking to your neighbours."

The three of them and Buddy walked down Oakley Avenue, pushing flyers through every letter-box and tying posters round trees and telegraph poles. As they reached the end of the street, they saw a young woman jogging along the pavement towards them.

"Does that lady live in your road?" Andi asked.

Will nodded. "That's Mrs Olson. She lives in this house here, with the green door."

Mrs Olson came to a halt as she reached Andi and the others. "Morning, Will," she said, leaning her hands on her knees to catch her breath. Her long dark ponytail swung forward over her shoulder. "What are you up to?"

Will showed her the posters and explained about Tiger. "Have you seen him recently?" he asked hopefully.

Mrs Olson straightened up. "I'm pretty certain I saw him last night," she said, to Andi's astonishment.

"You did?" Will gasped. "Where?"

Mrs Olson frowned. "Behind my house, I think, when I was taking out some rubbish. But I only caught a glimpse of him in the shadows beside the garages. It might not have been Tiger, but it was definitely a tabby cat."

"That's fantastic news!" Will exclaimed, turning to Andi and Tristan. "Isn't it?"

Andi was excited too, but she was also experienced enough not to put a great deal of hope on one sighting. "It's a good start," she agreed, smiling at Will. "We'll check the garages straight away."

They thanked Mrs Olson and walked on round the corner. Will punched the air with delight. "If Mrs Olson saw Tiger yesterday," he said, "that means he's still alive!" He was so happy, Andi

48

couldn't bring herself to tell him they might get several false sightings before they found one that really was Tiger.

They reached the end of Oakley Avenue with just one poster to spare.

"What next?" Will asked, looking hopefully at Andi and Tristan.

"Let's start asking questions," Andi said.

With so many people away on holiday, knocking on the neighbours' doors didn't take long. No one had a golden tabby cat locked in their garage, and there was no way of checking for pawprints in the gardens thanks to all the rain. After the excitement of Mrs Olson's news, it was a gloomy end to the morning.

"I really thought we'd find him, after what Mrs Olson said," Will said sadly, scuffing at the pavement with his trainer. "Mrs Olson probably didn't see Tiger at all, just some other tabby."

Andi tried to console him. "It's all part of the puzzle. You never know, it could be a vital clue later on." Privately, she suspected that Will's gloomy prediction was right after all.

After promising Will they'd phone if they heard any more news, Andi and Tristan headed down a long, straight avenue of grand-looking houses, discreetly placed behind hedges and tall fences. The trees that lined the road were stubbornly refusing to produce buds, and looked as cold and bare as they had at New Year.

Andi was just fixing a poster to one of the stately trees when her phone started ringing.

"Andi?" It was Natalie. She sounded breathless. "You've got to come over, now!"

"Why? What's happened?"

There was a pause, then Natalie said dramatically, "Andi – Rascal's gone missing!"

Chapter Four

There wasn't even time to finish tying up the poster. Andi bundled the string and paper back in her bag, tugged on Buddy's lead and waved frantically at Tristan, who was putting flyers through letterboxes on the other side of the road. "That was Natalie!" she called. "Rascal's gone missing!"

"What? When?" Tristan gasped, jogging beside her as they ran towards the Peterson's house.

"They couldn't find her after they got back from their shopping trip," Andi explained. "Poor Melissa. Poor Rascal! Can you imagine being that small and getting lost in a house as big as Nat's?"

They reached Natalie's road. "So you think Rascal's lost in the house?" Tristan asked.

Andi glanced at him. "Don't you?"

Tristan pulled a face. "What about Jet?" he said. "We've already seen him in action around that rabbit."

Andi shook her head. "I can't believe Jet would hurt Rascal," she said firmly. "Anyway, after yesterday, I'm sure Nat's being extra careful about keeping him in the dog room."

They ran up the path to Natalie's front door. The door opened just a crack before Andi had even touched the doorbell.

"I can't open the door any wider, in case Rascal's in here somewhere and gets out," Natalie explained through the narrow gap. She opened the door just enough for Andi and Tristan to squeeze inside, before shutting the door firmly behind them. "Melissa's really upset, because she thinks it's her fault."

"What happened?" Andi asked, putting Buddy in the dog room with Jet.

"Melissa was playing with Rascal in the games room, when her mum phoned from Hong Kong," Natalie reported. "Melissa went downstairs to take the call."

"And left the door open?" Tristan guessed. He sounded surprised. "I thought she'd be extra careful after yesterday!"

Natalie shook her head. "No, she closed the door but Maria was vacuuming the landing. The nearest plug is in the games room and she couldn't shut the door on the flex, so there was a tiny gap. I suppose that was enough for Rascal to escape, because when Melissa got back from the phone, Rascal had gone."

Tristan opened his mouth, but Natalie held up her hand. "If you're going to ask about Jet, you needn't bother," she said. "He was shut in the dog room the whole time."

There was a mournful bark from the far side of the dog room door when Jet heard his name.

"Is that Andi and Tristan?" Melissa called from the top of the stairs. She came halfway down and stopped. Her eyes were red and swollen, and she looked utterly miserable.

"Pet Finders to the rescue!" Andi declared. "Where should we start looking?"

"We've looked round the games room already,"

53

Natalie said, as they all trooped upstairs to join Melissa. "But we could check again."

"There are two options," Andi said briskly, pushing open the games-room door. "One, Rascal is still somewhere in the games room. Two, she got out through the gap in the door. The spaces behind the furniture in here are all blocked off, aren't they?" Natalie and Melissa nodded. "So when we finish checking in here, we should block off all the other small spaces around the house as soon as we've looked there," Andi said. "Lock cupboards after we've searched them, stuff like that. Just in case Rascal doubles back and hides where we've already looked."

Natalie went to the corner of the games room and pulled out a box of old vinyl records in square cardboard sleeves. "We could use these to block any gaps," she suggested. "Rascal couldn't jump over them."

After a thorough hunt around the games room to confirm that the little rabbit wasn't tucked behind the curtains or inside a cardboard tube, they began to move through the upper storey of the house.

Andi got down on her hands and knees to peer underneath the heavy curtains next to the windows on the landing. Beside her, Tristan checked behind a bureau, then blocked off the narrow gaps between the bureau and the wall, and the bottom of the bureau and the rug. They all gathered to search Natalie's bedroom, although Nat acted oddly when Andi wanted to look in her wardrobe.

"The door's been locked since before Rascal disappeared," she insisted. "There's no point wasting time in there."

They checked all the other rooms, cupboards and drawers, shutting every door firmly behind them. Then they repeated their search downstairs. At last, they ran out of places to look. Feeling gloomy, they slumped down on the sofa in the sun room.

"What if Rascal's got outside?" Melissa fretted. She looked through the window at the Peterson's spacious back garden. "She doesn't know how to survive outdoors."

Andi squeezed her arm comfortingly. "Don't worry about that yet," she said. "Rascal hasn't been missing long."

"We should put food in all the rooms, in case we can tempt her out of hiding," Natalie suggested.

Melissa pulled open the fridge and took out a bag of carrot tops. "Maria saved these from dinner last night," she said. "They're Rascal's favourite."

They each took a handful of the carrot tops, then walked round the house placing the food in the middle of each room. When they reached Mr Peterson's study, they found Maria vacuuming underneath the desk. Natalie put down the carrot top beside the door and tapped her on the shoulder. "Maria?"

Maria flipped the switch on the vacuum cleaner so the room fell silent. "You are still looking for the little rabbit?" she said sadly. "I am so sorry about what happened."

"It was really bad luck," Natalie agreed. "Could you stop cleaning for about half an hour? Rascal is more likely to come out of hiding if the house is quiet."

"Sure. I can go speak with John about the flowers for the party instead," said Maria. John was the Peterson's gardener.

"Let's wait in the kitchen," Andi said, as Maria went into the garden. "We can check the carrot tops after we've given Rascal a chance to smell them and come out from wherever she's hiding."

They tiptoed back to the kitchen, shutting the door as quietly as they could. Tristan headed straight for the fridge and made sandwiches for everyone. Then they sat and watched the kitchen clock.

"Have you ever found a rabbit before?" Melissa asked hopefully.

"We found Smokey," Tristan said at once. He had one of those memories that never forgot a thing. "Remember when all the animals in the pet shop went missing?" he reminded Andi and Natalie. "Smokey was the grey lop-eared rabbit that turned up in a building-worker's jacket."

Melissa's eyes stretched wide. "A whole pet shop of animals went missing? And you found them all?"

"Technically, the builder found Smokey," Andi admitted. They didn't have any direct experience of finding rabbits, she realized a little unhappily. She tried to remember if they'd had any similar cases to

Rascal. They had had a lot of trouble tracking down the school hamster once. The problem with small animals like guinea pigs, hamsters and rabbits was that they got scared really easily, and didn't come when you called their name. They were small, too, and moved extra fast. Not to mention the added danger from predators like foxes.

Andi sighed. None of these thoughts were very encouraging.

When they had finished the sandwiches, still only ten minutes had passed since they'd put the carrot tops down, so even though it was unlikely Rascal had got outside, they made a search of the back garden. As well as the generous sweep of lawn, there were lots of large shrubs and trees to check around – but there was no sign of Rascal anywhere.

When they came back inside, twenty more minutes had passed.

"Rascal's bound to have found the carrot tops by now, right?" Melissa said. Andi winced to see how hopeful she was – tempting a scared rabbit out of hiding with a few vegetable scraps was a bit of a long shot.

The first room they checked was the downstairs bathroom.

"I don't believe it!" Andi gasped.

The carrot top was gone.

"Rascal!" Melissa cried in delight, then clapped her hands over her mouth as Natalie and Tristan waved their hands and made shushing noises at her. They couldn't scare Rascal away now!

The hunt was on. Carrot tops were missing from the dining room, the snug, and the formal lounge. They raced upstairs. Sure enough, carrot tops were missing from the games room and Natalie's bedroom as well.

"How can Rascal be moving around the house so fast?" Tristan said in exasperation as they stared at the empty floor.

"Natalie? Melissa?" Mrs Peterson put her head round the bedroom door. "Can you explain what all these carrot tops are doing littered around the house?"

She had two carrot tops in her hands, holding them away from her as if they were contaminated. "I came in five minutes ago to see carrot tops all

over the house. There was absolutely no sign of Maria, so I've been everywhere, clearing them away. Can you please just feed Rascal in the kitchen in future? We must keep the house spotless for the party on Friday. I've had to cancel all my client meetings this week, because there's so much work to do. And carrot stains the pale rugs dreadfully."

"You cleared away the carrots?" Natalie said in dismay. "But we're trying to find Rascal, Mum! She's never going to come out if there's no food for her."

Mrs Peterson blinked. "Rascal's disappeared? Oh Melissa, I'm very sorry. I had no idea! Why don't we go into the kitchen and find some celery instead? Rabbits love celery, don't they?"

"And it won't stain the rug," Tristan murmured to Andi, as they followed Mrs Peterson to the kitchen. Melissa had gone very quiet and sad. It really did feel as if they were back to square one.

But the Pet Finders didn't give up that easily. They started again, this time putting chunks of celery all round the house. They decided to wait in Natalie's bedroom for Rascal to come out of hiding;

it was nearest the games room, so it made sense that Rascal had gone there first.

"We really should check your wardrobe, Nat," said Andi.

"No, wait—" Nat began, but Andi ignored her and reached for the key in the wardrobe lock. She turned it and pulled open the door.

"Help!" she spluttered, as jumpers, T-shirts and trousers tumbled out of the wardrobe and on to her head like a tidal wave of fabric.

Natalie looked embarrassed. "I told you not to bother," she said. "I can hardly get inside there myself, let alone Rascal. Oh!" She pounced on a pair of shoes that had fallen on to the top of the heap. "I've been looking for these for ages!"

"Why do you have so many clothes, Nat?" Tristan asked curiously.

"Oh, you know, some of us like to vary our outfits." Natalie stared pointedly at Tristan's red skateboarding T-shirt, which he'd worn practically every day that week.

After waiting a little while longer, the Pet Finders made another sweep of the house. The chunks of celery were exactly where they had left them. Either Rascal was too scared to come out of hiding – or she wasn't around to smell them.

"We've done as much as we can today," Andi sighed. "It's down to Rascal now. If she wants to come out, she'll come out."

"No Tiger, and now no Rascal," Melissa said sadly. "We're not doing much pet-finding today, are we?"

There was nothing Andi could say to disagree.

Andi was deep in a dream about catching Rascal. Every time she got close, the little rabbit gave one of her cute sideways kicks and leapt out of reach.

Suddenly the chase was interrupted by the bleep of a mobile phone. Sitting bolt upright, Andi snatched it up. "Nat?" she said, rubbing her eyes. "Have you caught her?"

"Hello?" said a quiet, elderly-sounding voice. "Is that the Pet Finders Club?"

"Sorry, I thought you were someone else," Andi said hurriedly. "Can I help you?"

"I hope so," said the voice. "My name is Mrs

Beryl Greenstreet. A neighbour of mine saw a flyer of yours, about a missing cat?"

"Yes, that's a case we're working on." Andi felt a tingle of hopefulness. "Have you seen Tiger?"

"I'm afraid not," Mrs Greenstreet said apologetically. "But there may be some kind of connection. I've lost my cat as well, you see, and I wondered if you might be able to find her for me."

"We'll do our best," Andi promised. Another case! Spring half-term was certainly a busy time for lost pets. She reached for a pencil and carefully wrote down Mrs Greenstreet's address. "We'll be over in about an hour," she promised.

As soon as Mrs Greenstreet hung up, Andi ran into the bathroom for a shower. Then she went to wake Tristan.

He sat up blearily. "Where's the fire?"

"No fire," Andi said. "But we've got another missing cat. Come on, get up!"

While Tristan had a shower, Andi called Natalie.

"There's still no sign of Rascal," Natalie reported, sounding tired. "Melissa and I were up until midnight searching for her."

"Was the celery still there?" Andi asked.

"Yep, every last piece." Natalie yawned. "We've put a bowl of rabbit food in the sun room today instead, in case Rascal likes that better."

Andi told her about her call from Mrs Greenstreet. "Why don't you bring Melissa?" she suggested. "It might take her mind off Rascal."

Natalie promised they'd be ready in half an hour. Andi checked a map to find Mrs Greenstreet's house. "It's not far from Will's, look." She showed Tristan. "We could make some house calls about Tiger afterwards."

Tristan looked down at the piece of paper where Andi had written Mrs Greenstreet's address. "Hey, I recognize this," he said. "Christine delivers cat food to this house on the first Thursday of every month. I don't think Mrs Greenstreet has ever come into the shop when I've been there, though. I'll phone Christine on the way and tell her we're going over there. She'll be really upset if Mrs Greenstreet has lost her cat."

Andi put Buddy on his lead while Tristan took his skateboard from the cupboard under the stairs, and they set off. Andi ended up jogging most of the way, partly to give Buddy a good run and partly to keep up with Tristan who was trying high-speed manoeuvres up and down the kerb. They reached the Peterson's house in double quick time, but luckily Natalie and Melissa were already waiting for them. Natalie held Jet on his lead, and the Labrador bounced around like a fish on a line when he saw Buddy running along the pavement.

"Thanks for coming with us," Andi said to Melissa. "You were great when we made that search for Tiger."

Melissa looked pleased and managed a faint smile.

It was a twenty-minute walk to Mrs Greenstreet's house – a neat white bungalow with a bench in the front garden where it caught the morning sun. They tied the dogs to the bench and rang the bell. The door was opened by a small, plump woman with curly, iron-grey hair. Her blue flowered blouse was neatly ironed and her feet were shod in comfortable-looking leather slippers.

"How kind of you to come," Mrs Greenstreet said after introductions had been made. She stood aside to let them in. "I'm getting very worried about Whiskers. She's been missing for several days now."

They walked into a cosy living room with a pink rug on the floor. There was a smart digital radio on the mantelpiece and a plate of biscuits stood waiting on the coffee table.

Mrs Greenstreet put her hand out and eased herself into a battered blue chair beside the fire. As Andi and the others sat down on the long blue couch opposite, she noticed Mrs Greenstreet was absently stroking a pink fleecy blanket folded over the arm of the chair.

"Whiskers adopted me about three months ago," the old lady began after Tristan invited her to tell them all about her pet. "I never really liked cats before, but then Whiskers came into my life and now I can't imagine what I'd do without her. We spend hours in here, listening to the radio. She's terribly lazy and spends most of her time curled up on her blanket, but that just makes her the sweetest, gentlest companion."

"Does Whiskers have any regular habits?" Melissa asked.

Mrs Greenstreet thought for a moment. "Well, I suppose she does the usual sort of cat things. She always comes in for her midday meal and then we spend the afternoon together. She's never around at night, so I suppose that's when she goes off catching mice. I don't like to interfere with her routine – if she wants to go out, then out she goes!"

"Have you got a photograph of Whiskers?" said Natalie.

Mrs Greenstreet gave a gentle smile. "I'm sorry, I haven't got any photographs at all."

Glancing round the cosy little room, Andi realized with a shock there wasn't a single photograph to be seen. "What does Whiskers look like?" she prompted.

"Well, she has the softest fur. And such long whiskers! They tickle me even when she's sitting some distance away. Oh, and her ears are very round and neat."

Andi frowned. It was an unusual description. "What colour is she?" she ventured. "Calico? Black-and-white? Tabby?"

"Brown tabby, I think," Mrs Greenstreet said.

"Do have a biscuit. I made them yesterday."

"When you say 'brown tabby'," Andi said, "do you mean—"

The kettle started whistling in the kitchen. Mrs Greenstreet stood up. "I'll be back in a moment. I expect you'd prefer a glass of juice to tea, wouldn't you?"

"Yes please," said Natalie and Tristan.

Andi followed her into the small tidy kitchen. "Can I help?" she offered. Glancing round the room, she noticed two bowls on the floor – one half-full of water, while the other had a few crumbs of cat food left at the bottom. There was also a cat bed underneath the window.

Mrs Greenstreet had lined up four glasses on the worktop and was pouring juice. There was something odd about the way she held the tips of her fingers just inside the rims of the glasses. It was as if Mrs Greenstreet could only judge how far she had filled each one by feeling the juice touch her finger.

Suddenly Andi understood.

Mrs Greenstreet was blind!

Andi rushed forward. "Can I help you with anything?" she asked. "It must be difficult for you, not being able to see. I mean . . ." She trailed off awkwardly.

Mrs Greenstreet stretched out her hand, found Andi's arm and patted it. "I can manage perfectly well," she said with a warm smile.

She carried the tray of glasses back into the living room and Andi watched her place it squarely on the coffee table, as if she could see perfectly.

Then something else struck Andi. No wonder Mrs Greenstreet had given such a curious description of her pet – she had never set eyes on her own cat! This was going to be one of their most unusual cases ever!

Chapter Five

"I never realized!" Tristan exclaimed in astonishment as they walked down the high street. "She didn't look blind."

"I know," Andi agreed. They were going to collect a cake from the Banana Beach Café. "She hides it really well, doesn't she?"

"How could a blind person describe her pet?" Natalie asked.

"Didn't you notice?" Andi said. "She described the way Whiskers *felt*. She described that brilliantly."

"But how does she know Whiskers is tabby?" Natalie persisted.

"Someone must have told her," Andi guessed.

"She didn't sound very interested in what

Whiskers looked like," Tristan said.

"I don't think Mrs Greenstreet is interested in what Whiskers *looks* like," Andi said. "Just what she *feels* like. Being blind, that makes total sense."

The cheerful awning and bright rainbow-coloured umbrellas outside the Banana Beach Café were a welcome relief from the heavy, colourless day. Dark clouds overhead rumbled ominously as Natalie pushed open the door.

"Bananas!" A blue-and-green parrot clicked its beak at them from a perch beside the counter. "More bananas!"

Melissa stared round, looking stunned. There were straw umbrellas over each table, and bunches of bananas hung on hooks above the counter. Pictures of white sandy beaches and aqua-blue water were placed around the walls, and reggae music pulsed softly from the stereo. "I feel as though I'm on holiday!" she gasped.

Andi laughed. "I know what you mean," she said, reaching up to stroke the parrot's glossy blue-and-green feathers. "This is Long John Silver," she told Melissa.

Buddy jumped up happily to greet the parrot. Long John Silver studied him with a wary eye, then clicked his beak and sidled as far away from the excitable terrier as he could.

Tristan looked at the pecan-and-banana muffins on display in the glass cabinet.

"No snacks," Natalie said firmly. "We're here to collect the cake Mum ordered for the party, and that's all. We've got three pets to find, remember?"

Tristan sighed theatrically and sank down at one of the café tables.

"Come to collect the cake?" Jango Pearce, a tall Jamaican man with grizzled hair, came out of the back room and smiled at them. "Maggie's just putting the finishing touches to it."

"Not as easy as it sounds when your son is trying to eat all the icing," Maggie Pearce declared, coming out of the kitchen with a large box. "Really, Fisher, how old are you?"

Fisher Pearce, the vet who ran the local RSPCA centre, followed his mother through the beaded curtain, licking his fingers. "Never too old for one of your cakes, Mum," he said.

"Hello, Fisher," Andi called.

Fisher grinned. "How's the pet-finding business?"

Natalie introduced Melissa, and they explained about Rascal and Tiger and Whiskers. Fisher whistled through his teeth. "Very busy, then," he commented.

"We're pretty sure Rascal's hiding somewhere in my house," Natalie told him. "What do you think?"

"That would fit with domestic rabbit behaviour," he agreed. "They like small spaces because it makes them feel safe from larger predators. Once she knows there aren't any foxes running around in your house, I'm sure she'll come out." He smiled at Melissa, who tried to smile back.

"And what about these cats?" Fisher prompted. "How's the search going for them?"

"There was a sighting of Tiger a couple of nights ago, but nothing since," Andi said. "We haven't started looking for Whiskers yet – we've only just spoken to his owner."

Fisher looked thoughtful. "Two cats missing within a few days? I don't like the sound of that. You could be dealing with catnappers, I'm afraid."

"What, someone deliberately stealing cats?" said Natalie, sounding surprised.

Fisher nodded.

"But Tiger and Whiskers aren't pedigree cats," Tristan pointed out. "Why would anyone want to steal them?"

"Well, you can make money from cats without breeding from them," Fisher said. "The thief might ask for a ransom, or perhaps sell the animals for their fur."

Melissa and Natalie gasped, and Andi gulped. "*Euw*," said Tristan. "They'd have to be horrible to do that."

"Thieves are horrible," Fisher said. "You should know that by now. Promise me you won't go looking for trouble?"

"Don't worry," Andi assured him.

"Good," Fisher said, looking relieved. "So, what's the plan? Running three cases at the same time must be pretty tricky."

"We've left food out for Rascal at home so we can look for Tiger and Whiskers this morning," said Natalie. She turned to the others. "Why don't we split into pairs, one pair to look for Tiger and the other to look for Whiskers?"

As they nodded, Fisher put in, "You could try asking if anyone else has lost a cat recently. Perhaps you could put up a notice about it in the corner shop. I'm sure Rachel would let you."

"Thanks for the advice, Fisher," Andi said, getting to her feet. "We'd better make a start. Oh!"

A loud clap of thunder made them all jump. Jet whined and retreated underneath Nat's chair, while Buddy jumped up and scraped at Andi's leg with his paw. Outside, the sky looked almost black and rain began pelting against the café windows.

"Did anyone bring an umbrella?" asked Natalie.

The others shook their heads.

"I hope Rascal isn't outside!" Melissa said anxiously.

Not just Rascal – Andi's stomach flipped over as she thought about the two lost cats, bedraggled and miserable in the rain.

"Looks like we're stuck here for a while," Tristan said. "Banana-and-pecan muffins for everyone, then?"

* * *

After half an hour, the rain showed no signs of letting up so Maggie lent them a large striped umbrella. At least they could keep the cake dry on the way back to the Peterson's house, although the umbrella was only big enough to shelter two people. Andi and Tristan volunteered to get wet, so Natalie and Melissa shared the umbrella, carrying the cake gingerly between them.

"You're soaked!" Mrs Peterson declared when she saw Andi and Tristan dripping on the porch. Apart from their trainers and socks, Natalie and Melissa were perfectly dry. "Come in and take off those wet things," she said. "Natalie can lend you some clothes."

"I don't need to borrow anything," Tristan said hurriedly.

"I'm sure Nat's got some non-girl stuff," Andi said. She shooed Buddy into the dog room and gave him a brisk rub with a towel. "Right, Nat?"

After a bit of grumbling, Tristan chose a crimson sweatshirt with a funky surf logo and some old jeans from the Peterson's charity shop pile that were a bit too short in the leg, while Andi opted for a pair of green silky combats, a lilac T-shirt and a blue cashmere jumper. While they were getting changed, Melissa rushed around the house to see if Rascal had eaten any of the food they'd left out – but everything was just as they had left it that morning. She was getting better at coping with the disappointment, but she still looked sad.

"We can't look for Tiger and Whiskers in this weather either," Tristan said gloomily, as they stood in Natalie's kitchen munching on cheese-and-tomato sandwiches. The rain was rushing along the guttering and pouring down the windows in small waterfalls. "They'll be even harder to track down if they've found somewhere out of the rain."

"Why don't we phone Will and Mrs Greenstreet, and tell them that we'll come over tomorrow?" Natalie suggested. "We can still split into pairs so we're covering both cases at the same time."

Andi took out her mobile phone and made the calls. Mrs Greenstreet was out, so she left a message on her answerphone. Will Jacobs picked up the phone on the second ring.

"Any news?" he said eagerly.

Andi felt a pang of guilt. "Not exactly," she said. "The weather's a big problem. If it's dry tomorrow, Tristan and I will make a start on the door-to-door enquiries. We need to widen our search." Andi knew she had to phrase her next piece of news carefully. "Listen, Will, we've got another missing-cat case," she said. "We're splitting up tomorrow to run two searches at the same time. I don't want to worry you, but there are signs we could be dealing with a catnapper."

"You mean, someone might have *stolen* Tiger?"

"Yes, I'm afraid so."

There was a pause. "Well, I suppose we shouldn't stop looking for him, just in case," Will said bravely. "See you tomorrow."

As Andi rang off, Mrs Peterson came into the kitchen. She was carrying an armful of snowy-white linen napkins. "Are you busy?" she asked.

They shook their heads. "Would you help me by folding these?" she said, placing the napkins on the table.

"The party's still two days away, Mum," Natalie pointed out.

"I know." Mrs Peterson pushed a hand through her shining blonde hair. "But it's all about preparation, and I've got so much to do. Now, where are my waterproofs? I'm trying to decide whether to use the greenery that grows by the back fence to decorate the stairs, but it might be quite wrong and I've got to make a decision today or the florist will never be able to supply what I need in time. Oh, this weather!"

Andi stared at the pile of napkins when Mrs Peterson had gone. "There must be a hundred of these," she said. How many people did the Petersons know!

"One hundred and four," Natalie replied, as her mum came back through the kitchen with a long waterproof coat and boots and disappeared into the sun room, where there was a door to the back garden. "I told you it was going to be a big party."

"Big?" Tristan echoed, reaching for an apple from the fruit bowl. "This is going to be like the Oscars!" He thrust the apple away in disgust. "Someone's taken a bite out of this already!"

He showed them a neat row of teeth marks in the side of the apple.

Melissa gasped. "They look like *rabbit* teeth marks!" she said, snatching the apple and gazing at the neat little grooves in the russet-coloured skin. "Shut the door, Natalie. Rascal must be in here!"

Everyone leapt out of their seats and stared round the kitchen. Natalie shut the doors to the hall and the sun room while Melissa started pulling open the cupboards. Andi and Tristan helped her, taking out cans and packets and putting them on the floor so they could see all the way to the back. Andi thought she spotted some rabbit droppings on the bottom shelf, but they turned out to be raisins.

When they'd emptied the entire larder, Melissa sat back and stared in frustration at the packets of food. "Those teeth marks must be Rascal's. She's *definitely* in here. But where?"

The sun-room door opened. Mrs Peterson stood in the doorway looking annoyed, her waterproofs leaving a puddle on the floor. "How many times," she sighed, "have I asked you to eat your breakfast in the kitchen, Natalie? You've made the most terrible mess in the sun room. The floor in there is bad enough already with all this wet and mud, and now there's cereal everywhere."

Natalie flushed. "Sorry, Mum," she said. She paused, then swung round to Melissa. "Did we have cereal this morning?"

Melissa frowned. "We both had toast, didn't we?"

Something clicked in Andi's brain. If the mess wasn't cereal, it must be . . .

"Rabbit food!" Melissa cried. "I forgot to check the bowl of food I left in the sun room!"

They rushed out of the kitchen and Andi and Tristan seized one end of the long wicker sofa while Melissa and Natalie took the other. They pulled it out from the wall. Behind it, Rascal's bowl of food was tipped on its side, scattering oat flakes across the floor. It looked a bit like muesli, which explained Mrs Peterson's mistake.

"Rascal must have started with the fruit bowl in the kitchen—" Natalie began.

"And then come in here!" Melissa continued, her eyes shining.

Andi felt a damp draught coming from behind her. The door leading out to the back garden was wide open.

"Mum, when did you open this door?" Natalie called to her mother.

"It's been open all morning," Mrs Peterson said, adjusting her coat and preparing to step outside again.

Andi stared at the others in dismay. This could spell disaster!

"Mum," Natalie said, making a visible effort to stay calm, "remember I told you that Rascal was missing? You shouldn't have left the door open! She might have escaped into the garden!"

"I'm very sorry about Rascal, but I've got to get everything ready for the party, Natalie," Mrs Peterson said gently. "The greenery won't sort itself out."

Melissa's eyes flooded with tears. "But Rascal doesn't know about being outdoors!" she said. "She'll be so scared!"

"There's no point worrying about that now," Andi said, before Melissa broke down completely. "We'll just have to look outside again. Come on."

They kitted themselves out with waterproofs and headed outside. The rain had lessened, but it was still falling softly. Andi surveyed the garden. They'd made a brief sweep the day before, but now it looked as if Rascal really had got outside, it was time to get more focused. Where to start? The shrubs suddenly looked very big, full of potential hiding-places for rabbits.

"Let's use the dogs," Natalie suggested.

"No! If they find Rascal, they'll scare her!" Melissa wailed.

"We'll put them on leads," Andi promised. "It's a great idea – we can use their noses to sniff out Rascal's trail."

Jet was overjoyed to be let out of the dog room, and it took Natalie several minutes to calm him enough to put on his extendable lead. Buddy's lead didn't extend, but it was long enough to allow him to sniff among the bushes. Holding tightly to the leads, Andi and Natalie led the dogs outside, with Tristan and Melissa following close behind. Melissa carried a tub of dry rabbit food, which she shook as she called Rascal's name.

"We should quarter this end of the garden, closest to the house first," Andi decided. "If Rascal's never been outside before, I think she'd head for the nearest hiding-place."

They started walking slowly across the lawn. Jet ran in circles, his nose to the ground and his tail wagging madly, while Buddy pulled Andi towards a bed of shrubs. Jet yelped and hurtled after them. Soon, both dogs were sniffing excitedly at the largest bush.

The thicket of glossy green leaves was too dense to see underneath just by lifting the outer branches. Andi stared at the muddy soil at the base of the shrubs. There was just enough space for someone to wriggle through on their stomach.

"Time for one of us to get dirty," she said. "Tris?"

"Why me?" Tristan protested.

"You're always a bit grubby," Nat said. "Anyway, you said you didn't like the clothes I lent you, so it won't matter if they get muddy."

Tristan plucked at the crimson sweatshirt underneath his coat. "It's growing on me," he said.

"Go on," Andi pleaded. "Nat and I are holding

85

the dogs, so we can't do it – and Melissa's a guest Pet Finder, so we can let her off the muddy stuff. Pretend you're doing army training or something."

"I may be gone some time," Tristan sighed, hitching up the legs of his jeans and hunkering down. "If I don't come out, tell Dean he can have my stereo—"

"Get on with it!" Andi said, giving him a nudge. Tristan lowered himself on to his belly and inched under the leaves. Soon, all they could see were his feet. Andi held her breath, imagining the little rabbit cowering and frightened in the damp and the shadows.

"We're coming!" she called softly. "Don't worry, little one. You'll soon be safe!"

Chapter Six

"Can you see anything?" Melissa called.

"*Euw!*" Tristan wriggled backward out of the shrubbery in a rush, his face screwed up and mud all over him. "There's a dead pigeon under there. That must be what the dogs could smell. Sorry."

Melissa's shoulders slumped and Natalie went over to comfort her. Andi hunkered down and tried to look underneath the leaves. "How did it die?"

"I didn't ask it." Tristan looked as if he felt queasy. "I think something had been eating it."

"What, like a fox?" Andi said without thinking.

With a horrified cry, Melissa wrenched away from Natalie and ran back to the house in tears. Andi, Tristan and Natalie looked at each other.

"If there's a fox around," Natalie said grimly, "then Rascal doesn't stand a chance."

She tugged on Jet's lead and followed Melissa into the house. Andi and Tristan continued quartering the garden, just in case. The rain steadily grew worse and the daylight began to fade. They decided to abandon the search and make a fresh start the following day.

Melissa and Natalie were sitting at the kitchen table, slowly folding napkins. Melissa's eyes were red and puffy.

"The good news is that there's no sign of a rabbit in the garden, dead or alive," Andi announced, trying to sound cheerful for Melissa's sake.

Melissa sniffed, and a tear rolled down her nose and plopped on to one of the napkins. "I miss her so much," she whispered. "She's so little and helpless."

Andi and Tristan's clothes had been put through the dryer and were folded neatly on the kitchen table, waiting for them. "We'd better get changed," Tristan said to Andi, "and then we've got to go. Dean's making cheese straws shaped like fours and zeroes for the party, and we'd better check he's not including any weird ingredients."

"Fours and zeros?" Natalie echoed.

Tristan beamed. "To spell out your stepdad's age," he said. "Good idea, isn't it? Listen, try and stay positive, Melissa. Remember what Fisher said, about rabbits liking small spaces? Why would Rascal choose a big wet space like the back garden when there are plenty of small dry ones inside the house?"

"I'll ring you tomorrow, Nat," Andi said. "We've still got two cats to find, remember?"

"A day of pet-finding might keep us all from brooding about Rascal," Tristan added. "Imagine if we find both Tiger and Whiskers tomorrow! Stranger things have happened."

Andi felt a bit more hopeful. As Tristan was fond of saying, tomorrow was another day.

To Andi's relief, the next day was brighter and it had stopped raining at last. Flinging back the quilt, she reached for her mobile phone to ring Natalie. The phone rang while she was scrolling down for Nat's number.

"Andi?" It was Natalie. "You've got to get over here, fast!"

"Have you found Rascal?"

"Not yet, no," Natalie said. "But we went out to the garden early this morning to see if we'd missed any clues yesterday, and we saw this man in next door's garden."

Andi was hopping round the room trying to pull on her clothes with one hand. "So why do I have to come over right now?"

Natalie lowered her voice. "I know for a fact that Mr and Mrs Holland are away, so what's a stranger doing in their garden?"

"It does sound like the kind of thing Fisher told us to look out for," Andi agreed. "But we're looking for a catnapper, not a rabbitnapper, aren't we?"

"That's just it!" Natalie sounded triumphant. "Mr and Mrs Holland *have got two cats*. Valuable ones, too. I think they're Burmese or something."

Andi's heart started thudding. This could be a really important lead. "Don't try to speak to him!" she warned Natalie, hurrying across the landing to bang on Tristan's bedroom door with her free hand. "We'll be over as soon as we can."

News that they could be hot on the trail of the catnapper made Tristan leap out of bed and pull on his clothes in double quick time. "We'll ask Mum for a lift," Tristan said as they raced downstairs.

Andi jumped the last two steps. Just as she landed, her mobile phone started ringing again. This time it was Will Jacobs.

"My dad's had to go out, but he said he'd be back later this morning," Will said. "Mum's home and ready to help with the search. What time are you coming round?"

"How about eleven o'clock?" Andi suggested. "We've got to investigate a man who's been seen near Natalie's house, but we'll come over straight after that."

"What man?" Will demanded. "Do you think he's the catnapper? Hey, I'll come too! At Natalie's house, you said? Where's that?"

"Don't get too excited, Will," Andi warned him, but she gave him Natalie's address. "And we'll need to be really careful if we do suspect him of being a thief."

"I'll cycle over right away," Will said, then hung up.

"The Pet Finders Club has never had so many members!" Tristan remarked.

Mrs Saunders looked up as they entered the kitchen. "There are waffles on the table if you want them," she said.

"Thanks, Mum," Tristan said. "Could you give us a lift to Natalie's house?"

"If you're ready to go in approximately thirty seconds," Mrs Saunders warned.

Andi and Tristan raced through their breakfast, fed the animals, brushed their teeth and combed their hair in just under two minutes. Luckily Mrs Saunders was still waiting for them, jingling her car keys.

"Natalie and Melissa have seen someone acting strangely in the neighbours' back garden," Tristan explained as his mum steered the car out of the driveway. "We're looking for a catnapper at the moment, and he sounds as though he could be a suspect."

"Don't approach him on your own," said Mrs Saunders. "I haven't got time to come in now, but I'll ring Mr Peterson when I get to the office and ask him to go with you."

Tristan rolled his eyes. "Why do adults think we'll get into trouble all the time?"

"It's because we know you too well," Mrs Saunders replied. She pulled on to the Peterson's driveway.

"Thanks for the lift, Mrs Saunders," Andi said, as Buddy scrambled to get out of the car first. "We promise not to get into trouble, OK?"

Melissa opened the front door, looking even sadder and paler than the day before. Andi realized she'd been so excited about the new catnapper clue that she'd forgotten how bad Melissa must be feeling. Rascal had been missing for two nights now.

"Did you see any sign of Rascal in the garden?" she asked.

Melissa wiped her eyes. "We found some tufts of fur, but they were the wrong colour and not soft enough. Natalie thought they might belong to the Hollands' cats."

Andi wondered uneasily if two cats could kill a small rabbit. She had a terrible feeling that the answer was yes. Especially if the Hollands' cats were Burmese, as Natalie said. They had a reputation for being ferocious hunters, often bringing down birds as big as themselves.

"We found rabbit pawprints too," Melissa continued, as they walked into the kitchen, "though they could have been made by wild rabbits."

Andi put her hand on Melissa's arm. "I lost Buddy when I first moved to Aldcliffe," she said, "and Tristan lost Lucy for almost six months. Nat even lost Jet once. I know it's hard to stay positive, especially when we're following up a clue that doesn't have anything to do with Rascal. But I promise we all know how you're feeling."

"Thanks," Melissa said, trying to smile.

The sun-room door clattered and Natalie came into the kitchen. "He's still there!" she announced. "He's got a ladder propped against the side of the Hollands' house! Suspicious or *what*?"

"Is your stepdad around, Nat?" Andi asked.

"I've already asked him to come with us if we go

next door," Natalie said promptly, guessing what Andi was going to say next. "He's ready to go as soon as we like."

Andi squared her shoulders. If this man was the catnapper, they had to catch him quickly. "Let's go now," she said.

Mr Peterson was a tall, easy-going man with a deep tan and eyes that crinkled in a friendly way when he smiled. He worked from a home-office three days a week, so he was often in when Andi went over to Natalie's house. Today, he appeared from his study when Natalie knocked on the door, and together they walked along the road to the Hollands' house. They left both the dogs at Natalie's house, in case they barked and gave the thief a warning that someone was coming.

Like the Petersons, the Hollands had a house built in an old-fashioned style with leaded-light windows and a neatly-mowed front garden. The driveway was empty, which wasn't surprising as the Hollands had gone on holiday.

There was a squeal of bicycle brakes and Will Jacobs hurtled up. "I came as quickly as I could!" he puffed. "Have you confronted him yet?"

Natalie introduced Will to her stepdad. "Confrontation won't be necessary," Mr Peterson said. "This man is probably here for a perfectly good reason. The first thing we're going to do is ring the front doorbell."

Tristan looked aghast. "You might scare him away!"

"Geoff, you're not taking this seriously," Natalie complained to her stepdad.

"There's no way out of the back garden except through the side gate." Mr Peterson indicated a black gate at the side of the house. "We'll see him straight away if he makes a run for it. You kids stay here." He walked up to the front door and rang the bell.

Will tugged Andi's sleeve. "Why don't we look round the side of the house?"

Tristan nodded. "If this man's going to try a getaway, we need to be ready."

"You watch too many police shows on TV," Andi told him.

"We should stay here, like Mr Peterson said," Melissa added.

"My stepdad can still see us," Natalie pointed out. "We're not going through the gate or anything. We could just have a peek."

Natalie was right. The side gate was in full view of Mr Peterson, who was still standing in the front porch. Natalie creaked open the gate and peered inside.

"He's still there," she whispered. "He's putting a ladder against the back of the house!"

"Let me have a look!" Will pushed forward to see past Natalie.

"Dad!" he gasped. "What are you doing here?"

Chapter Seven

Mr Jacobs climbed down from the ladder. Wiping his hands on his overalls, he strode across to the gate. "Will?" he said. "I thought you were out looking for Tiger this morning."

"I don't understand," Natalie said, sounding utterly confused.

Andi didn't understand either. If Mr Jacobs was the catnapper, why had he taken his own cat? Perhaps he stole Whiskers and then took Tiger as a cover! How many more cats had he taken? A thousand thoughts and suspicions tumbled round her head.

"We thought, er," Tristan stammered, "we thought that . . ."

Mr Jacobs pulled a notebook out of his back pocket and jotted something down. "How's the pet-finding going, you two?" he asked, glancing at Andi and Tristan. He hadn't met Natalie before, but he obviously remembered them from their first visit to Will.

"The Hollands want me to give them a quote for fitting air-conditioning before the hot weather kicks in," Mr Jacobs went on, putting his notebook away. "I thought I'd have a look at the outside of the house for an initial assessment while they're away. Is there some kind of problem?"

Everyone shook their heads. It was far too embarrassing to explain to Mr Jacobs that they'd thought he was a thief!

Mr Peters came through the side gate. "I take it you're not a thief?" he said dryly, extending his hand and introducing himself to Will's dad.

"A thief?" Mr Jacobs exclaimed. "What am I supposed to have stolen?"

"Cats," Tristan said, a little helplessly.

On cue, the cat-flap in the Hollands' back door rattled and out came two beautiful Burmese cats,

one a darker shade of chocolate than the other. Andi held out her hand and the darker brown cat reached up to butt its head softly against her palm.

"My, what a crowd!" A woman in a tracksuit appeared in the open gate. Her face cleared when she saw Mr Peterson and she gave Natalie a wave.

"That's the Hollands' neighbour on the other side," Natalie whispered to Andi. "Mrs Molloy. She feeds the cats when the Hollands are away."

"Hello again, Mr Jacobs," said Mrs Molloy, fishing around in her tracksuit pockets until she produced a key to the back door. The cats tangled themselves around her legs, meowing in distinctive bass voices. "Nearly finished with the air-conditioning estimate? I'll lock the gate when I've fed the cats, if that suits you."

Mr Peterson looked interested. "You do air-conditioning?" he said to Will's dad. "That's a coincidence. Our system was making this awful clacking noise last year which drove us all mad. I expect you get pretty booked up in the summer, so would you be able to have a look for me when you've finished here? We're next door."

"No problem," said Mr Jacobs. "I'll be over as soon as I can."

"Well, *that* was embarrassing," Tristan muttered, as they walked back to Natalie's house.

"You don't need to tell me," Natalie muttered back.

Will looked utterly downcast, and Andi wondered if he was cross that they'd mistaken his dad for a thief. But then he said sadly, "Perhaps Tiger hasn't been stolen. Perhaps he just didn't like us any more and ran away."

"Cats don't run away unless they've been treated badly," Andi said. "I'm sure Tiger knows how much you love him. We'll find him soon, Will."

"At least we can cross your dad off the list of suspects," Melissa put in.

"List?" Andi sighed. "If only!" Once again, they were back at square one.

As they walked into the Peterson's hallway, which was now festooned with greenery for the party, Melissa stared in dismay at the door to the dog room. It was open and there was no sign of Jet or Buddy.

"The dogs have escaped!" she gasped.

"Don't panic!" Andi instructed.

They immediately started checking the rooms downstairs. Mr Peterson, who had followed them back from next door, found Buddy sniffing around in his study, but there was no sign of Jet.

"Hang on, I've got an idea," said Andi. She dragged Melissa towards the kitchen, thinking it was best to keep her busy while the others went on searching. "The only thing Jet's really interested in, apart from walks and stuff, is food. Real food, not rabbits," she added hastily.

There was no sign of Jet in the kitchen, but Andi heard snuffling coming from the sun room. Natalie, Tristan and Will came running when Andi called, and together they rushed into the room to see Jet's black rump sticking out from underneath the wicker sofa. His tail was wagging so fast, it was a blur against Mrs Peterson's tasteful pink and green soft furnishings. He'd obviously found something very good under the sofa. Melissa went white.

Natalie crouched down and peered underneath.

"It's OK, he hasn't got Rascal! He's just after the bowl of food."

They heaved the settee away from the wall and Natalie grabbed Jet by the collar. Rabbit food was scattered across the tiles and once again the little dish was tipped over. It all looked horribly familiar.

"Oh no," Andi gulped. "What if it was Jet who ate the food yesterday?"

There was a pause as this sank in.

"It means we could have been following a false trail," Tristan said at last.

Andi didn't dare look at Melissa. How would she react to yet another piece of bad news?

"But if Rascal didn't get as far as the sun room, she might not have gone outside after all!" Melissa pointed out.

Andi nodded. "If it was Jet who ate the rabbit food last time, it does look like Rascal could still be inside."

"Those rabbit teeth marks in Tristan's apple are still a great clue," Natalie reminded everyone. "Jet's teeth are much bigger and he'd never steal food from the worktop. Rascal must definitely have

106

been in the kitchen some time after she went missing."

But where was she now? Andi wondered.

The doorbell rang.

"That'll be Dad," Will guessed. Sure enough, Mr Jacobs was standing on the porch with a bag of tools slung over his shoulder. He glanced round at the decorations in the hallway. "Is someone having a party?"

Mr Peterson, who had come out of his study at the sound of the doorbell, rolled his eyes. "Don't ask," he said.

Mrs Peterson emerged from the living room, two enormous glass vases tucked underneath her arms. Her husband introduced Mr Jacobs. "I've been meaning to get someone round to look at the air-conditioning," she said. "I heard reports of some unseasonally hot weather due at the end of the week. But there's so much to do when you're expecting over a hundred guests! Mr Jacobs, you and your family must come along tomorrow night!" She swept out of sight and through to the kitchen.

"Over a hundred guests?" Mr Jacobs echoed in astonishment.

Mr Peterson said nothing.

"Aren't you looking forward to the party, Geoff?" Natalie sounded a bit hurt.

"Of course," her stepdad said hastily.

"It'll be worth all the preparations," Natalie promised.

"It had better be," Tristan said gloomily. "Mum's lined up a really itchy suit for me to wear."

The only formal dress in Andi's wardrobe was a red one she'd last worn at a Christmas party two years ago. She hoped her mum didn't expect her to wear that. It was at least two sizes too small.

"Where would you like to start?" asked Mr Peterson, looking at Will's dad.

Mr Jacobs looked up at the high ceiling in the hallway, then squatted down to peer along the skirting boards. "Just looking for vents," he explained, noticing Andi's curious gaze. "I'll need to have a look at the original architect's drawings," he went on to Mr Peterson as he took an electronic gadget from his bag and swept it across the wall.

Every now and again, the gadget gave a little bleep. "These houses often have very complex systems and, although this tells me roughly where your pipes are, I'll need a copy of the plans before I can check all the vents."

"My architect's busy today – I tried to get hold of her about something else earlier – but she should be able to come up with something for you tomorrow." Still talking, Mr Peterson led Mr Jacobs through to his study and shut the door.

Andi checked her watch. It was nearly eleven o'clock. "Time to look for Tiger and Whiskers," she said. "Tristan, you and I can make enquiries around Will's house. Nat, you and Melissa can take Mrs Greenstreet's."

"But I wanted to look for Rascal," Melissa began.

"I know it's hard," said Natalie, "but if she's indoors, I promise she'll be safe for a bit longer. It would be really helpful to have you on the search this morning." Andi could tell she wanted to keep Melissa busy so she didn't worry herself to distraction.

"OK," said Melissa. "But please can we look for Rascal this afternoon?"

"Definitely," Natalie replied.

Mrs Peterson bustled back into the hall. This time, she was carrying silver candlesticks, two in each hand. "Would you have time to fetch some dog food from Paws for Thought this afternoon, Natalie?" she asked. "I just haven't had time to get any this week."

"OK," said Natalie.

Outside the sun was shining weakly, though it still didn't feel much like spring. "Paws for Thought is halfway between our two locations," Andi said, "so let's split up now and meet up there in a couple of hours."

"Perfect," Natalie said. "My stepdad always tells me that the key to getting stuff done is good time management. Good luck – hope you find Tiger."

"Same for you and Whiskers!" Andi called as Natalie and Melissa set off along the road with Jet straining to break free from his extendable lead.

Buddy sniffed his way along the pavement as Andi, Tristan and Will went in the opposite direction.

Will's mum had left a note to say that she'd been

called out unexpectedly and wouldn't be back in time for the search after all. Will left his bike on the porch and followed Andi and Tristan as they searched the local streets. They saw a couple of cats (the wrong colour for Tiger) snoozing on porches and, where families had gone away for half-term, unmowed lawns and letterboxes stuffed full of post. Without the accompanying noise of traffic, lawn mowers and other normal neighbourhood activity, Andi realized she'd never heard so much birdsong before. Wherever they spotted cars on driveways or letterboxes without newspapers stuck halfway out, they knocked on the front door and asked if anyone had seen Tiger. One or two people recognized Will's cat, but no one had seen him in the last few days. By the time they reached the last road, Andi's feet were sore and her heart was heavy. It was tough, not turning up a single clue. She checked her watch. It was nearly one o'clock.

"Sorry, you two, but we've run out of time," she sighed. "We'd better head for Paws for Thought or the others will wonder where we are."

Natalie, Melissa and Jet were waiting for them

when they reached the pet shop. Andi took one look at the dejected way that Natalie was leaning against the shop window and knew they hadn't had any luck either.

"There was hardly anyone to ask," Natalie said. "It feels as though the whole town is away on holiday."

"How did Mrs Greenstreet take the news?" asked Andi.

"She was very brave about it, although you could tell she was disappointed," Melissa said. "I know how that feels. Knowing your pet is out there somewhere, but not knowing where, is awful."

"I'm not even looking forward to the party any more," Natalie said gloomily. "What if all the guests scare Rascal and she goes even deeper into hiding?"

It was better than thinking of Rascal outside facing a fox, Andi decided, remembering the dead pigeon. But she didn't want to upset Melissa so she said nothing.

When they went into the pet shop, Christine's friendly cocker spaniel, Max, ambled over to greet them. Jet and Buddy followed him to his favourite spot in the window and lay down as if their paws were tired out from all the searching.

Christine Wilson was talking to a couple and their little boy, who looked about six years old. "You'll need a warm basket, two litter trays, and I would recommend this brand of cat food," she was saying, holding a can of tinned meat. "I'd keep the cat indoors for several days, just until he gets used to his new surroundings."

Andi's ears pricked up. A cat with a new home? Christine wasn't recommending kitten food, so it was clearly an adult cat.

With a meaningful glance at Andi, Tristan walked up to the counter.

"Hello, Christine," he said. He smiled at the customers. "Did I hear you talking about a new cat?"

"Yes, that's right," said the man. He was tall and broad-shouldered with pale blond hair. "Have you got a cat, too?"

Tristan nodded. "She's a silver tabby called Lucy."

"Tabbies are gorgeous," the little boy's mother agreed.

Andi felt a flicker of excitement. Did that mean

their new cat was tabby, too? If so, it could match Tiger's description!

"Did your cat, er, just turn up one day?" Tristan asked casually.

"Tristan?" Christine said. Andi noticed a touch of steel in her voice. "Would you go and fetch me a box of budgie treats from the storeroom?"

Tristan looked surprised. "What, now?"

"Yes, now," Christine said firmly. "I won't be a moment," she said to her customers. "Feel free to have a look at the pet beds."

"Uh-oh," Andi muttered, following Christine and Tristan to the back of the shop. Natalie, Melissa and Will pressed close behind her.

Christine was standing in the storeroom with her hands on her hips. "I can't have you badgering my customers!"

Tristan looked mutinous. "I was doing some important detective work!" he argued. "We're looking for two adult cats. I overheard them talking about re-homing an adult cat. It's natural to ask questions!"

Christine folded her arms. "You weren't asking

questions," she said. "You were laying traps. The Donaldsons got their cat from an elderly man who's going into an old people's home. I arranged for them to give the cat a new home."

"Oh," said Tristan.

"We didn't mean to upset your customers," Andi said quickly. "We're just running out of ideas for finding Tiger and Whiskers."

"I'm sorry to hear they're still missing, really I am, but I don't think you'll track them down like this." Christine ushered them all out of the storeroom. "I promise I'll let you know if I hear of any recently re-homed cats, OK? Now, I've got to get back to work."

They bought Jet's dog food and trooped outside feeling very downcast.

Andi summoned a smile from somewhere. "This isn't the end of the search, Will," she said. "We've got to go back to Natalie's now because we promised to look for Rascal this afternoon, but we'll keep looking for Tiger as well, don't worry."

Will sighed. "Call me later, yeah?" he said. "I'd better go and find Dad, and make sure no one else has mistaken him for a burglar. Thanks for everything. I know you're trying your best."

He trudged away with his head down and his hands shoved in his pockets. Andi sighed. Why was pet-finding always so difficult?

Back at Natalie's house, they ate a quick lunch of chicken salad before planning the next phase of looking for Rascal.

"The last clue we had was the spilt food in the sun room," Andi said.

"And the teeth marks in my apple in the kitchen," Tristan put in.

They headed for the sun room first. Andi checked the wicker settee itself, feeling along the underside and the arms in case a tuft of rabbit fur had caught into the weave. When they found nothing, they returned to the kitchen. The food that Melissa had put out earlier was untouched.

Tristan picked up an apple and weighed it in his hand. "I've just had a weird thought," he said. "How did Rascal get that apple?"

Andi frowned. "What do you mean?"

Tristan indicated the fruit bowl which was sitting on the counter. "The fruit bowl was up here. I know rabbits can jump, but could a rabbit really jump all the way up here from the floor?"

"Could Rascal have used the kitchen chairs?" Natalie suggested.

Melissa shook her head. "Even the chairs are too high for her."

It was a puzzle. Andi checked the rest of the grey marble work surfaces, working her way steadily around the kitchen. There was a bowl of freshly-washed lettuce standing by the sink. A single leaf had fallen from the bowl and was sitting temptingly on the draining board. Either this lettuce leaf had frilly edges – or something had been nibbling it.

"Look at this!" Andi called, her heart suddenly beating faster.

Melissa grabbed the leaf and stared at it. "Rascal's been here again!"

"This is impossible," Andi said in frustration. How had Rascal got from the games room to the work surfaces in the kitchen? And how could

Chapter Eight

Apart from the nibbled lettuce leaf, there were no other clues in the kitchen.

"Melissa, where else did you leave food?" Andi asked.

"I put lettuce in the bathroom and the living room downstairs, and the games room and Nat's room upstairs."

"Let's start in the downstairs bathroom," Tristan suggested. "It's closest to the kitchen."

They piled into the small bathroom and shut the door. Then, with mounting excitement, they stared at the piece of lettuce Melissa had left below the sink. Half of it was missing.

"Rascal's been in here too!" Andi exclaimed.

"So where is she now?" Natalie said, staring round the empty room.

"Stop pushing," Tristan grumbled. "I'm squashed against the bath."

"That's nothing," Melissa squeaked. "Natalie, you're pressing me against the radiator!"

Andi moved aside the shower curtain to the shower cubicle and stepped inside. It was a relief to find a bit of space. "OK, it's a bit small to have all of us in here," she said. "You two check in here for gaps or holes. Tristan and I will go and look in the living room."

Tristan wiped his forehead as he and Andi slipped back into the hall. "Phew! That was a bit too close to a shelf of hair products for comfort."

Mr and Mrs Peterson were in the formal lounge, discussing table plans for the party. They looked up as Andi and Tristan ran in and shut the door swiftly behind them.

"Rascal's left a food trail!" Andi said. "She's definitely been in the kitchen and the downstairs bathroom." She looked round and spotted another lettuce leaf under the window. Unlike the one in the bathroom, this leaf was intact.

"Rascal's been in both the kitchen *and* the downstairs bathroom?" Mrs Peterson echoed in surprise. "Why hasn't anyone seen her?"

"We've been wondering the same thing," Tristan admitted. "Somehow she's sneaking around the house, totally unseen."

"It sounds as though she's using some kind of cloaking device," Mr Peterson said with a smile.

"We thought she might be teleporting," Tristan said solemnly. "But Melissa thinks that's pretty unlikely."

Mrs Peterson stood up and pushed the table plan to one side. "Come on, Geoff, let's start looking," she declared. "I don't want Rascal popping out of the woodwork during the speeches. It would be far too distracting. Andi, have you checked the top cupboards in the kitchen yet?"

Andi shook her head. "Just the larder and the cupboard with saucepans," she said.

"I'll have a look myself," Mrs Peterson offered. She cocked her head. "Can you hear a mobile phone?"

Andi recognized her mobile ringtone pealing faintly from the hall. She rushed out and grabbed it out of her jacket pocket.

"Hello? Is that Andi?"

"Hello, Mrs Greenstreet," Andi said, recognizing the old lady's voice. "Is there any news about Whiskers?"

"I've been out with my neighbour this afternoon – she's the one who helps with my shopping and other chores. We've covered several more roads," Mrs Greenstreet replied. "We met a number of very friendly cats along the way, but none of them *felt* quite right."

"I know what you mean," Andi said. "Buddy's coat feels like nothing else on earth. I'd know him just by the rough patch between his shoulders."

"I do miss her." Mrs Greenstreet sounded sad. "It's silly, I know, but my armchair doesn't feel right now Whiskers isn't sitting next to me. I've started sitting on the sofa instead."

Andi looked up as Natalie and Melissa came clattering down the stairs. Natalie waved her arms and mouthed something at Andi. "Um, Mrs

Greenstreet?" Andi said, "will you excuse me a moment?" She covered the receiver with her hand and raised her eyebrows at Natalie.

"Invite Mrs Greenstreet to the party!" Natalie said out loud. "You never know – one of the guests might have seen Whiskers."

Andi went back to the phone. "Natalie wants to ask if you're busy tomorrow evening, Mrs Greenstreet."

"Well, no." Mrs Greenstreet sounded surprised by the question.

"Would you like to come to a party?" Andi asked. "At Natalie's house? You can meet some more of your neighbours and perhaps we could ask if anyone has seen Whiskers in their gardens or garages. There are more than a hundred guests coming."

"Gracious me. We could ask lots of questions, couldn't we?"

"You'll have a captive audience," Andi agreed, encouraged by the lift in the old lady's voice. "So, will you come? The RSPCA vet, Fisher Pearce, lives near you so I could ask him to give you a lift."

"Yes, I know Fisher," said Mrs Greenstreet. "That would be lovely, thank you. I'll be there."

"Thanks for that suggestion, Nat," Andi said, clicking off the phone. "Are you sure your mum won't mind?"

Natalie shrugged. "What's one more guest when we've already got so many?"

In the kitchen, Mrs Peterson was studying the leaves of a pot plant with a puzzled expression on her face.

"Doesn't that plant usually live above the plate rack, Mum?" Natalie asked.

"Yes," Mrs Peterson said with a frown, turning the pot in her hands. "It's very peculiar. Look at this." She showed them the leaves of the plant. They had very clearly been nibbled.

"Rascal!" Melissa squeaked, staring at the nibbled leaves in excitement.

Andi stared up at the shelf above the plate rack. It was a long way from the floor. "How did Rascal get on to that shelf?" she said in confusion.

"Rascal's a terrific jumper," Melissa said proudly.

"She'd need to be a terrific pole-vaulter to get

right up there," Tristan pointed out.

Mrs Peterson pulled off the nibbled leaves and set the plant back on its shelf. "Why don't we leave out more lettuce tonight?" she suggested. "I'm sure we can spare some. Even a bit of radicchio, if that would help."

"Great idea, Mum," said Natalie, and she told her about inviting Mrs Greenstreet to the party.

"What a lovely idea," said Mrs Peterson. She glanced at her husband, who was reading the paper at the kitchen table. "You don't mind, do you, Geoff?"

"Nothing to do with me," Mr Peterson grunted.

Mrs Peterson looked shocked. "It's everything to do with you, Geoff! It's *your* party!"

Mr Peterson glanced at Andi and raised his eyebrows ever so slightly. Andi had to suppress a giggle. The party on Friday night might *technically* be for Mr Peterson's birthday, but it was pretty clear who the real host was.

Andi and Tristan were surprised to find that Tristan's parents were both home early.

"Hello," Tristan called, putting his keys on the hall table and bending down to make a fuss of Lucy, who was twining round his ankles and purring loudly.

"We thought we'd make an effort to be back for dinner tonight," Mrs Saunders said, coming out of the kitchen. "We couldn't go away for half-term this year because we're so busy in the office, but we've hardly seen you or Dean or Andi, and half the week's gone already! Lasagne and home-made garlic bread are in the oven."

As the entire Saunders family, plus Andi, sat down for dinner, Andi thought how nice it was being in the middle of a big family for a change. She loved living with her mum, but their mealtimes were never this lively. Buddy snoozed by her ankles, his head on her feet as usual.

Tristan was updating Dean and his parents on their latest pet-finding problems. "Both cats and the rabbit are still missing," he sighed. "It feels as though we haven't got anywhere, and we've been searching all week."

"I'm sorry, Tristan," said his mum. "It must be really frustrating."

"I could drive you round Aldcliffe tomorrow," Mr Saunders offered. "Our assistant is looking after the office and I haven't got anything else to do."

"Oh yes you have." Mrs Saunders waved her fork at her husband. "Sorry, Tris, but I need your father tomorrow. The garden is looking like a jungle and I need him to dig out the flowerbeds – if we can find them. By the time we've finished, we'll have the tidiest garden in the street."

"That won't be hard," joked Dean, reaching across for the last piece of garlic bread. "Everyone else has abandoned theirs for half-term. Oi!" Tristan had beaten him to the garlic bread, placing it triumphantly in the middle of his plate.

"Oh!" Andi gasped.

Tristan looked at her in surprise. "What?"

"We've been looking at this all wrong," Andi said excitedly. "People go away at half-term, right? So what if Tiger, or Whiskers – or both – have got themselves locked in a garage, or a shed, or something? No one would be around to let them out. We've been asking all the people who *haven't* gone on holiday about Tiger and Whiskers, when we should be checking the garages and sheds of the people who *have*!"

"So we aren't looking for thieves any more?" Tristan asked. He looked a bit disappointed.

"It's still a possibility," Andi said. "But this seems more likely. Don't you think?"

"I guess you're right!" Tristan spun round to his mum. "Can we go and check tonight?" he pleaded. "Oakley Avenue isn't all that far, and—"

"Tomorrow," Mrs Saunders said gently. "It's gone half past seven and too dark now."

"First thing tomorrow?" Tristan pressed.

"OK. On one condition."

Tristan looked wary. "What?"

His mother reached for the garlic bread on his plate. "That I can have this," she said, and she popped it in her mouth before Tristan could protest.

The morning of the Peterson's party dawned bright and warm. It looked as though the unseasonal warm weather Mrs Peterson had mentioned was starting bang on time. After Andi had made a call to Fisher asking him to give Mrs Greenstreet a lift to the party that night, she and Tristan headed for Oakley Avenue again.

"We need to look for *empty* houses this time," Andi said. "Unswept paths, overflowing letterboxes, that kind of thing. I'll phone Nat and arrange to meet at the Peterson's house. We could do another split search, like before."

But Natalie and Melissa weren't going anywhere. "Rascal's been in my stepdad's study!" Natalie told Andi. "Mum put some radicchio in there last night and it was half eaten this morning. Don't ask how the rabbit got in there. My stepdad swears he left the door closed all night."

Night-time, Andi thought, as she dialled Will's number to tell him about the new search. *Perhaps Rascal's moving around in the dark, when everyone's asleep?* Perhaps they should plan a sleepover and stake out the house in the dark.

Mr Jacobs answered the phone and told them that Will had an orthodontist appointment that morning and wouldn't be able to help. Without Natalie, Melissa or Will, Andi and Tristan faced a long day of searching on their own, but that wasn't going to put them off.

They decided to start with Whiskers and Mrs Greenstreet.

"The garages are round the back of the houses, here," Andi said, showing Tristan the map as they stood by Mrs Greenstreet's front door. "If you go round that way while I take this path, and we spiral outward like this" – she swirled her finger in an expanding circle round the map – "we'll meet at this point here." She indicated a large house on a corner plot. "Remember to check for signs—"

"—of unoccupied houses, yes, I know." Tristan flapped his hand at her impatiently as he started down the road.

Andi ran after him and thrust a pile of Pet Finders Club flyers in his hand. "Just in case the neighbours want to know what you're doing," she reminded him. Then she set off down the overgrown path which ran alongside Mrs Greenstreet's house and into a quiet alley lined with garages.

Half the garages had no glass in the windows,

meaning a cat would be able to get out on its own, and the rest looked dark and quiet when Andi hefted herself up and peered through the glass. The sheds were all locked securely, silent and empty-looking. Determined to pace herself and not overlook anything, Andi moved slowly down the row of garages, then turned back and did the same on the other side of the lane. After a while the garages and sheds started to blur into one another, until she wasn't sure if she was checking the same garages twice.

"Absolutely nothing," Tristan reported bleakly when they met up. "Apart from an old man who threatened to set his dog on me, until I produced one of our flyers and explained what I was looking for. You?"

"The same, minus the old man with a dog," Andi sighed.

They walked despondently back to Oakley Avenue. Even the bright sunshine and unusual warmth did nothing to cheer them up. Andi stopped to peer over the fence of an empty house, while Buddy sniffed at the bottom of the posts.

"The family's not at home!" a voice called to them from across the street. "Can I help?"

Andi turned and saw Mrs Olson watching them from her open front door. Beside her stood a little girl of about four.

"You're Will's friends, aren't you?" said Mrs Olson. "Are you still looking for that cat?" Andi nodded. "I wondered what you were up to, peering through the Mancinis' hedge. You can't be too careful at this time of year. Burglars love to find a road full of empty houses."

"Meow," said the little girl and hid behind her mum's legs.

"Good pussycat," Mrs Olson said, stroking her daughter's head and winking at Andi and Tristan. "We've just been to visit Katie's grandma," she explained. "She's got a Siamese cat, and Katie's been pretending to be a cat ever since."

The little girl peeped out from behind her mum's legs and meowed again. Tristan meowed back, making her giggle.

"Do you think your neighbours would mind if we checked their sheds and garages?" Andi asked.

"Go ahead," Mrs Olson said. "If anyone asks what you're up to, tell them I'll vouch for you, OK? Good luck." She turned and went back into the house.

Her daughter, Katie, stayed on the porch. She pointed to the empty house where Andi had been looking over the fence. "Meow," she said again, looking hopefully at Tristan.

"Woof woof," Tristan barked, and the little girl shrieked with laughter.

"Pussycat run away!" she squeaked. "Naughty dog!" She pointed again at the empty house. "Grandma's cat," she said.

Next to the shuttered house was a shed tucked into a corner of the front garden. It was almost hidden beneath a tangle of brambles and it was clear it hadn't been used for a long time.

"Your grandma lives there?" Andi said.

Katie shook her head. "Grandma's cat," she said.

"Your grandma's cat?" Andi said, looking again at the shuttered house with the darkened shed. "Did you hear your grandma's cat over there, Katie?"

"Woof!" Tristan barked again, and the little girl giggled and ran inside.

"Tris!" Andi said, annoyed. "Why did you do that? I was asking Katie a serious question!"

"It was just a game," Tristan protested.

"Shh!" Andi said suddenly, tilting her head on one side.

"What's eating you?" said Tristan grumpily.

Andi whirled round. "Katie's been hearing a cat all right," she said in excitement. "But not a Siamese like her grandma's. Siamese cats meow almost as though they're talking – it's unmistakable. But listen to that!"

In the silence, they both heard a scrabbling sound from deep inside the darkened shed across the road, followed by a long, wailing, very un-Siamese-like meow.

Chapter Nine

Andi raced into the garden, Tristan close behind her. Sensing their excitement, Buddy yipped and capered round their feet.

"Aren't we trespassing?" Tristan panted, as they skidded to a halt outside the shed.

"Mrs Olson said she'd vouch for us if anyone asked," Andi said, looping Buddy's lead round a heavy flowerpot to leave her hands free. She stared up at the shed window, which was loosely propped open at the top so that there was a small gap between the window and the frame. Andi jumped up at the gap, trying to avoid the brambles round the base of the shed.

"There's definitely a cat in there!" she declared.

Tristan grabbed the door handle. "Locked," he said, twisting it left, then right. They both heard the cat scrabbling again, deep inside the shed.

"Is there any way we can get through the window?" Tristan asked, staring at the dusty pane of glass above their heads.

"It's too small," Andi replied. "Besides, we'd scratch ourselves to bits on those brambles if we fell." She spotted a tree with sturdy branches overhanging the shed. "The cat must have jumped in through the window from one of those branches and then couldn't jump out again," she guessed.

Tristan tried tugging at the door of the shed again.

"Kick it," Andi suggested.

"We don't want to break it!" Tristan protested. "Mrs Olson won't vouch for us doing that. Anyway, we'd scare the cat. Let's phone my dad."

Andi frowned. "Why would your dad be able to open the door any more easily than we can?"

"My parents keep so many keys for all their properties, maybe Dad'll have a key that fits."

Mr Saunders promised he'd come over as fast as

he could. "He sounded pretty keen," Andi commented, snapping her mobile phone shut.

"I expect releasing cats from sheds beats digging flowerbeds," said Tristan, squinting up at the sun. "Especially now it's getting warm."

They settled down with their backs against the door of the shed. Andi made soothing sounds and sang little songs through the door to the trapped cat, in case it was frightened. Buddy whined when he heard her voice and tugged at his lead, so Andi shifted round so she could stroke his tummy at the same time.

Mr Saunders arrived in less than ten minutes. Parking the car, he jumped out carrying a bag that jingled loudly. "I brought as many as I could find," he said, dumping the contents of the bag on the grass beside the shed. He picked a small bronze key from the pile and tried to fit it in the lock. He jiggled it about, but it wouldn't go in all the way.

There was a frantic scrabbling sound on the other side of the door. If it was one of the missing cats, it had been shut in that shed for the best part of a week and would be very hungry, maybe even traumatized. Andi peered up at the partially-open window. With all the rain of the past week, at least the cat should have got a little water to drink. She put her eye to a tiny gap in the side of the shed and tried to peep inside. She could just make out the cat's silhouette, but nothing more. Was it Tiger? Or Whiskers? Or some other cat altogether?

"Try this one, Dad," Tristan suggested, handing over a slightly smaller key. Mr Saunders tried again, leaning his head against the door to listen for the telltale click of an opening lock.

"It's like robbing a bank," Tristan said, as his dad discarded the second key and chose a third.

"Except we're not stealing anything, we're setting something free," Andi reminded him.

Tristan waved his hand impatiently. "Details, details."

"This isn't working," Mr Saunders sighed, straightening up from his fourth attempt on the lock. "It looks as though we'll have to get the real key from somewhere."

"Looking for these?"

They turned to see Mrs Olson standing in the

driveway behind them, dangling a key-ring between her fingers.

"Perfect!" Andi gasped.

"The Mancinis always leave a set of keys with me when they go away," Mrs Olson said, fiddling with the key-ring. "When Katie came inside and told me about the game she'd been playing with you, I thought perhaps you'd found something." She detached the smallest key and handed it to Andi. "Try this," she suggested.

Andi put the key in the lock and carefully turned it. There was a smooth clicking sound. Cautiously, she turned the handle and tugged the door open. A tabby-coloured blur shot out.

Andi leapt to her feet and flung herself on the frightened cat, pinning it to the grass, where it struggled and spat beneath her.

"Shh, it's OK . . ." she soothed, trying to avoid the cat's flashing claws. At last she managed to get a firm grip and started stroking the cat's head. The cat stopped struggling, but its ears were still flat to its head as if it was waiting for its chance to escape. It was dusty, but its tabby markings and white tummy were clear. Gorgeous golden tabby stripes stretched along its body. There was no sign of a collar.

"It's pretty fat for a cat that's gone without food for a couple of days," Mr Saunders remarked. "And it doesn't look as if it's been hurt. Is it one of the cats you're looking for?"

Andi checked. "It's a tom," she said. "And Will did say that Tiger was fat." She gazed in delight at the cat in her arms. They had found Tiger! Will was going to be so pleased!

Tristan unwrapped his jacket, which he'd tied to his waist, and folded it round the cat to stop it from struggling. "Let's go and see if Will's in!"

"It'll be time for the party soon," Mr Saunders reminded them as he climbed back into his car. "You're both sleeping over at Natalie's, aren't you?"

The party! Andi had forgotten all about it. It was already past four o'clock and the party was due to start at seven. Her mum was coming home at six, and she had to get back and change and—

"Earth to Andi." Tristan's voice interrupted her thoughts. "Let's go and reunite Will with Tiger!"

It was hard not to run up the road with excitement, but Andi and Tristan walked as carefully as they could to avoid scaring Tiger any more. Tristan held his jacket as though it contained fragile glass as Andi rang the bell.

There was no answer.

"They must still be at the orthodontist," Andi realized. "What should we do? We can't leave Tiger here. He's hungry and scared. He could run off again."

"Let's take him back to Natalie's," Tristan suggested. "The Jacobs are coming to the party tonight, aren't they? We can reunite them there."

Andi phoned home to leave a message for her mum, explaining that she was going straight over to the Peterson's and asking her to bring her party outfit and overnight bag. Andi's heart sank as she realized she'd have to wear her red dress from last year; she'd been so busy looking for Rascal, Whiskers and Tiger that she hadn't had a chance to look for a new outfit.

The Peterson's house was almost unrecognizable. Twinkling white lights were strung across the front of the house, and a wreath of spring flowers and gold-sprayed branches hung in the porch. Men in blue overalls were carrying chairs and boxes of wine into the house from a row of vans parked outside. Tristan held Tiger carefully as he and Andi picked their way through the bustle of party preparations in the hallway.

"You've found Tiger!" Natalie recognized the beautiful striped tabby at once. "That's fantastic? Why have you brought him here?"

"Will's not in," Andi explained. "Can we put Tiger somewhere here where he'll be safe?"

"How about my bedroom?" Natalie suggested, stroking the cat's soft furry head.

Tristan took Tiger upstairs while Andi put Buddy in the dog room with Jet. The terrier immediately curled up next to the black Labrador, who barely raised his head as Andi pulled the door shut. It looked as though the dogs were getting used to their new Rascal routine.

"Where's Melissa?" Andi asked as they made their way upstairs with a bowl of water and a can of sardines for Tiger. The banisters had been wrapped in ivy and it felt a bit like climbing a tree.

"Staking out the games room again," Natalie replied. "I'm getting pretty worried about her, actually. I can't even get her interested in her party outfit."

"I wouldn't be able to think about a party outfit if Rascal was my pet," Andi admitted.

Natalie looked crushed. "I know what you mean," she said, "but it's such an amazing outfit – we found it the other day. It's this gorgeous little turquoise . . ." She stopped herself. "Anyway, you'd think it might cheer her up a bit. I don't think Rascal's going to come out tonight anyway, not with all these people around."

They found Tristan in Natalie's bedroom, brushing dust and cobwebs out of Tiger's fur. "Do you think Melissa will mind me using Rascal's grooming brush?" he asked.

"Probably," Natalie said tartly, reaching down to take the brush from Tristan, "if it *was* Rascal's grooming brush. But that's my hairbrush."

Melissa came into the bedroom. She stopped dead at the sight of Tiger drinking thirstily from the bowl of water. "What's that cat doing in here?" she gasped. "What if Rascal sees him?"

Andi stopped wrestling with the can of sardines. She hadn't considered that. It was getting more and more complicated, keeping all these animals away from each other.

"We'll put him in the garage," Natalie decided, as Tiger started meowing hopefully at the smell of sardines. "He might get scared with all the people in the house tonight."

They trooped back down with Tristan carrying Tiger again. Mrs Peterson was straightening a floral arrangement on the hall table. "Andi, I've had a message from your mother," she said. "She got home about twenty minutes ago, and she's coming straight over with your outfit, OK? Oh! Is that a cat?"

Natalie explained about Tiger. "We thought he could go in the garage, just until his owners arrive," she said.

Mrs Peterson looked relieved. "Yes, the garage would be a good place," she said. "I don't think we could cope with another animal in the house tonight." She fanned herself with an elegantly-manicured hand. "It's warming up, isn't it?" she said. "Rather pleasant for this time of year, but with a house full of people this evening, we might need to call on the air-conditioning a little earlier than usual. It would be great if Geoff could get it fixed before our guests arrive. Mr Jacobs will be here soon, so perhaps he'll have some ideas. What do you think of these flowers, Natalie? Are they a bit . . . floral?"

"Aren't flowers supposed to be floral?" Tristan whispered to Andi, as they left Natalie and Melissa with Mrs Peterson and took Tiger through the inside door to the garage. Andi bit her lip to stop herself giggling.

"Will was right about Tiger liking sardines," she commented, watching the golden tabby tuck into the bowl of fish they had put on the floor. "I don't think he's even chewing them!"

"I hope Rascal doesn't turn up in here tonight," Tristan said. "Tiger would terrify her."

"We'll keep the door firmly shut," Andi decided.

"That doesn't seem to help," Tristan pointed out.

"Remember how Rascal got into Mr Peterson's study, even though he closed the door?"

"Well, it's the best we can do," Andi said firmly. "Until we work out how Rascal does it, we'll just have to keep doing the logical thing and shut the doors."

Tiger finished the sardines and sat down with his tail curled neatly over his paws. He looked up at Andi and Tristan with his gorgeous amber eyes and opened his mouth in a loud meow.

"Are you feeling a bit better?" Tristan asked. "Hey, Andi, remember how Will said he loved playing with that toy mouse?" He found a roll of string on a shelf and waved the end in front of Tiger. The tabby pounced, his long striped tail whisking back and forth as he chased the string across the floor. "You'll be home with your elastic mouse soon, old chap," Tristan promised, bending down to smooth Tiger's fur.

Andi couldn't help thinking about Mrs Greenstreet's gentle cat, Whiskers, still lost somewhere in Aldcliffe. She hoped their luck would hold out long enough to find her, too.

They left Tiger on a folded blanket in a corner of the garage. Then Tristan headed home to change while Andi went to look at the dining room. It was swagged in white, yellow and gold fabric, and sprays of white flowers sat in the middle of the long table on the far side of the room. Amid several tempting plates of appetizers, Mr Peterson's birthday cake took pride of place on a golden stand, with curly white ribbons tumbling artistically from the top of the icing. It looked very striking, but Andi wondered how much of it was to Mr Peterson's taste. It was his birthday, after all.

"Hello, Andi! Have you missed me?"

Andi whirled round to see her mum standing in the doorway, wearing a shimmery lilac dress. "Mum!" she cried, rushing over to give her mother a hug. "How was the conference?"

Mrs Talbot hugged her back. "Useful but dull," she said. "I would much rather have been at home with you and Buddy. Mind you, from what I hear I wouldn't have seen you, with all the pet-finding you've been doing this week. Right, are you going to get changed now?"

"Mum," Andi began, as she followed her mum out of the dining room, "about my outfit. I don't think I fit into it any more."

"How do you know?" teased Mrs Talbot, leading Andi into the snug. "You haven't even seen it yet."

Andi gasped when she saw the clothes draped across the settee. There was a pair of dark-blue satin combats, cropped just below the knee, and a stretchy, long-sleeved dark-blue top decorated with a scattering of plain white crystals. Flat blue pumps stood on the floor. "It's *gorgeous!*" she said, when she could speak. "Thank you so much, Mum!"

"Quick, go upstairs and put it on," said Mrs Talbot, smiling.

Andi hugged her again, hard, before running upstairs to change. If only they'd managed to find Rascal and Whiskers, this party would have been perfect!

Chapter Ten

Among the first guests to arrive, on the dot of seven o'clock, were the Jacobses. Mr Peterson promptly dragged Mr Jacobs into his study to talk about the air-conditioning.

Andi, feeling fantastic in her new clothes, rushed up to Will. "You won't believe it," she grinned at him, "but Tiger's here!"

Will looked astonished. "You mean, in this house?"

"Yup, right here," Tristan confirmed, appearing behind Andi.

Natalie and Melissa joined them as they led Will to the garage. Melissa looked pale and sad, but Andi was pleased to see Natalie had persuaded her to put on her party clothes. The turquoise dress suited her and put a little colour in her cheeks.

Will pushed open the door to the garage and peered inside. There was a deep, rumbling meow of welcome and the sound of a cat jumping lightly down from the counter.

"Tiger!" Will scooped up the purring tabby cat and held him close. "It's really you!"

Andi felt her eyes misting up.

"Thank you so, so much!" Will said, looking over Tiger's head at the Pet Finders. "Mum and Dad will be totally amazed that you found him. Where was he?"

Andi and Tristan took turns describing Tiger's dramatic rescue. Aware of how Melissa must be feeling, Andi was careful to keep the story short and had to tread on Tristan's toe every now and again to stop him from embellishing it too much. She could imagine what it was like for Melissa, seeing Will so happy when she was still feeling so miserable about Rascal.

They left Will to get re-acquainted with Tiger, and wandered back through the house. Nearly all the guests had arrived by now and were standing round in their best evening clothes, talking and laughing and holding crystal champagne glasses. The Thai-style appetizers were disappearing fast; Andi caught sight of Tristan watching mournfully as a woman with long scarlet fingernails took the last fishcake.

Mrs Peterson rushed up to them, magnificent in full-length red satin. "Natalie, have you seen your stepfather? Everyone's here, but there's no sign of him."

"From pet-finding to people-finding," Tristan said promptly, dragging his gaze away from the empty plate. "We'll find him, Mrs Peterson. Don't worry."

"I got the impression your stepdad wasn't looking forward to the party," Andi whispered to Natalie, as they squeezed through the crowded downstairs rooms looking for the guest of honour. "Perhaps he's run away."

"He wouldn't do that," Natalie decided. "He knows it would cause way too much trouble with my mum. Er, Tristan? My stepdad won't be in the broom cupboard."

Tristan reversed out of the cupboard and dusted down his jacket. "Sorry," he said. "I went into pet-finding mode there."

"Was there any sign of Rascal in there?" asked Melissa. "I put some lettuce leaves behind the door earlier."

Tristan shook his head. "Sorry, there were some leaves but they didn't look like they'd been eaten."

They carried on hunting for Mr Peterson. It felt strange to be searching for a person in Natalie's house, rather than a rabbit. Andi resisted the urge to block off all the small spaces they passed.

As they turned the corner on the upstairs landing, there was an odd thumping noise above their heads.

Tristan looked up at the ceiling. "What's up there, Nat?"

"Just the attic," Natalie said. "But my stepdad wouldn't—"

They turned the corner and came face to face with Mr Peterson and Mr Jacobs descending the wooden attic ladder. Mr Peterson looked happier than he had all week.

"Geoff!" Natalie gasped. "Your suit! Mum's going to totally kill you!"

Mr Peterson looked down at his cobwebby dinner jacket, and picked off a couple of dead spiders that were dangling from the hem of his jacket. "As we were upstairs, I asked Mr Jacobs about installing air-conditioning in the attic," he said, looking sheepish. "I've been thinking of converting it into a bedroom. It's a terrific space, and . . . Anyway, what have I missed?"

Natalie dragged her stepfather to the nearest bathroom. "You've nearly missed all the appetizers!" she said disapprovingly, sponging down his dinner jacket before bustling him down the stairs.

"You'll be lucky to find any fishcakes," Tristan grumbled under his breath as he and Andi followed.

Over the heads of the guests gathered in the hallway, Andi saw Mrs Greenstreet standing in the porch with Fisher Pearce and Christine Wilson.

Andi ran downstairs to give them the good news. "We found Tiger! Will's with him now, in the garage. Fisher, do you think you could quickly check him over to make sure he's OK?"

"You found Tiger?" Mrs Greenstreet sounded pleased. "That's very good news. Will must be delighted."

"Yes, he is. We found Tiger in a locked shed," Andi explained, letting Mrs Greenstreet take her arm and then leading her, Fisher and Christine through the crowds. "Now that we know what to look for – houses where people have gone away for half-term – we'll be starting the search for Whiskers again tomorrow, in case the same thing's happened to her."

Christine took Mrs Greenstreet through to the kitchen while Andi escorted Fisher to the garage. They found Will sitting cross-legged on the floor. Tiger was standing on his hind legs, batting at the roll of string. He looked pretty fit for a cat who'd been stuck in a shed.

"Will, this is Fisher," Andi began.

Suddenly there was a loud scrabbling noise outside the garage door. To Andi's horror, two wet black noses shoved the door fully open, sniffing eagerly. Jet and Buddy had escaped from the dog room!

"I'm so sorry!" A woman in a dark-blue dress rushed up behind the dogs. "I was looking for the downstairs bathroom and accidentally let the dogs out . . ."

Will let out a yelp as Tiger dug his claws into his lap and then launched like a tabby-coloured rocket straight past Fisher and Andi, out of the garage and into the house. Jet and Buddy whirled round and hurtled off in pursuit.

"Quick!" Andi gasped.

Tiger streaked through the kitchen with Jet and Buddy hot on his tail. With one monumental effort, Andi flung herself at Jet and sneaked a finger through his collar, bringing him to a screeching halt in the doorway to the sun room. Will skidded to a halt just behind her. Meanwhile Fisher scooped Buddy up with one hand.

Mrs Greenstreet was sitting on the wicker sofa with Tiger trembling in her arms.

"Thanks, Mrs Greenstreet!" Andi panted. "If Tiger had made it into the back garden, we could have lost him again!"

Mrs Greenstreet ran her hand over the terrified,

fluffed-up cat. "Tiger?" she echoed. "This isn't Tiger. It's Whiskers!"

"No, this is my cat, Tiger," Will said.

"Tristan and I found him today," Andi added.

Mrs Greenstreet shook her head. With her fingers, she gently followed the contours of Tiger's ears. "I promise you this is Whiskers," she said calmly.

A cheer went up from inside the dining room. Andi guessed Mr Peterson had made his entrance at last. Tristan, Natalie and Melissa came out of the dining room and walked through the kitchen, Natalie with her arm firmly linked through Melissa's. They all stopped in the door to the sun room, clearly sensing the peculiar atmosphere.

"What's going on?" Tristan asked, looking round.

"Mrs Greenstreet has just told us that Tiger isn't Tiger," Fisher announced. "He's Whiskers."

Tristan opened his eyes wide in astonishment.

"But Mrs Greenstreet, this can't be Whiskers!" Natalie protested. "Tiger's a tom cat and you said Whiskers was a girl."

The beautiful tabby cat was sitting on Mrs

159

Greenstreet's lap with its eyes half closed. There was no sign of the playful, energetic cat they'd seen in the garage with Will. Instead, this was a very gentle pet, who wasn't going to rush round and demand busy games. It was almost as if he knew Mrs Greenstreet couldn't see and needed a special kind of stillness.

"I'd know that purr anywhere," Mrs Greenstreet said with a smile. "I must confess, I only *assumed* Whiskers was a girl. Everyone was always telling me how pretty she was, you see. They must have figured she was a girl just from the way she – or he – looked. What a mix-up!"

Andi glanced at Will, who was looking devastated. They'd all been so sure it was Tiger – Will most of all. That was the weird part. Surely an owner wouldn't mistake the identity of his own cat?

Then, like the sun breaking through a cloud, something occurred to her. Was it possible that this cat was Tiger *and* Whiskers?

"Tristan, go and fetch that roll of string from the garage, will you?" she said. "I've got a theory I'd like to try out."

When Tristan returned with the cord, Andi took it and waved it in front of the sleepy cat. Immediately he pricked up his ears.

"Oh!" Mrs Greenstreet gasped as the cat leapt off her lap and raced after the cord, his claws skittering on the tiles. "Is Whiskers playing?"

"It *is* Tiger," Will said, grinning broadly. He scooped the cat off the floor and sat down next to Mrs Greenstreet. The cat immediately rolled on to his back and started batting at Will's fingers.

Andi looked at Fisher, feeling totally confused. "Is it possible for a cat to have a split personality?"

Fisher nodded. "Cats often reflect the behaviour of their owners," he said. "Will is young and energetic, while Mrs Greenstreet leads a quieter life. It's clear that this cat loves them both equally, and adjusts his behaviour according to the person he's with."

Suddenly Tiger stopped playing. He padded along the settee and nudged his head very gently against Mrs Greenstreet's arm. As soon as the elderly lady moved her hand, the cat snuggled down beside her and rested his head on her knee.

He looked as if running around was the last thing he'd want to do.

Andi watched the transformation from playful Tiger to docile Whiskers with a mixture of delight and alarm. It was fantastic to think they'd solved two cases at once – but if Tiger and Whiskers were the same cat, what were Will and Mrs Greenstreet going to do now?

"I don't understand," Melissa said, looking from Will to Mrs Greenstreet and back again.

"You're not the only one," Natalie muttered.

"No wonder he's so fat," Tristan declared. "He's been getting fed twice!"

Fisher leant down and palpated Tiger gently. "Hmm," he said with a frown. "He's quite overweight. We might have to put him on a special diet. The extra weight may have helped him when he went without food for a few days, but it's very dangerous in the long term and can cause diabetes and liver disease. We'll talk about it later, Will – I mean, Mrs Greenstreet . . ." He broke off. "Who should I be talking to here?"

Andi was wondering the same thing. They'd

never found a cat with two owners before. If Tiger and Whiskers were the same cat, who actually owned him?

"How long have you had Tiger, Will?" Mrs Greenstreet asked.

"Nearly three years," Will replied.

"Then he's yours," Mrs Greenstreet said simply. "Whiskers – Tiger, I mean – only came to me a few months ago."

Will ran his hand along Tiger's back and looked thoughtful. "I don't mind sharing him," he said at last. "I mean, I've been sharing him for ages, haven't I? I just hadn't realized."

"Are you sure?" Mrs Greenstreet's face broke into such a delighted smile that Andi felt tears pricking behind her eyes. "If you can really spare him, I would love that. I'll try to remember to call him Tiger. When Andi and Tristan told me you'd lost your cat, they said he had beautiful gold stripes. Is that where his name came from?"

"Yes," said Will. "He's got really unusual gold-and-chocolate fur."

Mrs Greenstreet beamed. "It's lovely to be able

to picture her – I mean, him – properly. My neighbour just described him as tabby, so I had an idea in my head that he was a mix of brown and grey. I had a brown-and-grey tabby when I was a girl, you see. But I'm surprised no one recognized him from your posters and realized Tiger and Whiskers were the same cat!"

"The picture on Tiger's poster was very small," Will explained. "He never stayed still long enough for me to take a photo." He grinned down at the tabby, who was lying as still as a statue on Mrs Greenstreet's lap. "I suppose he saved his quiet time for when he was with you!"

Melissa sniffed, as if she was struggling not to cry. Andi felt a wave of sympathy for her.

Mr Peterson came out of the dining room with Mr Jacobs.

"Where are you going now?" Natalie asked her stepdad. "You can't keep running away from your own party!"

Mr Peterson looked defensive. "We've checked the vents upstairs and we need to do the same down here. Your mum wants the air-conditioning on

164

before we cut the cake. With so many people in the dining room, it's getting a bit stuffy."

"My stepdad is hopeless," Natalie muttered, watching them disappear. "If he gets his dinner jacket dirty again, Mum is going to be furious. He'll be gone more than half an hour, I know it. Those vents are everywhere."

Will and Mrs Greenstreet were working out Tiger's feeding programme. "How about if you feed him in the morning, then we have him for his evening meal?" Will suggested. "Feeding him's always a rush in the morning for me because I have to get ready for school."

"Will's being so cool about this," Tristan whispered to Andi. "I could never share Lucy."

"I couldn't share Rascal either," Melissa said miserably, overhearing. "That is, if I ever find her again."

Andi glanced round the sun room. Where *was* that little rabbit? If only they could second-guess Rascal's next move and lie in wait for her. How was she managing to pop up all over the house without anyone seeing her? She was small, but not that small!

As Will bent down to put his cheek against Tiger's, Melissa let out a strangled sob and rushed out of the sun room. Andi, Natalie and Tristan followed her up the stairs to Natalie's bedroom, where she had flung herself down on the bed.

"I've walked up and down this corridor a hundred times," she wailed. "If I just knew where Rascal was hiding, at least I could wait in the right place. She's got to come out sometime, hasn't she?" She broke into a fresh storm of crying.

"Of course she has," Andi said. "You've just got to be patient." But it was hard to keep on reassuring Melissa when they were no closer to solving the mystery of the disappearing – and reappearing – runaway rabbit.

Melissa blew her nose. "It's OK," she said, in a small, sad whisper. "I know what you're all thinking." She swallowed. "I'm never going to see Rascal again, am I? She's gone for ever, and she's not coming back."

Chapter Eleven

There was a knock on the bedroom door.

"Natalie?" It was Mrs Peterson, looking flustered. "Have you seen your stepfather anywhere? I really would like the air-conditioning on in the dining room now. We can't cut the cake without the guest of honour! Honestly, you would think this was my party, not Geoff's at all . . ." She broke off as she noticed Melissa's red eyes and blotchy face. "Oh, poor you," she said, more gently. "Still no news of Rascal?"

Melissa shook her head miserably. "I hope you don't mind, Mrs Peterson, but I think I'll skip dinner," she said. "I'm not very hungry."

"I'll get Maria to bring you up a plate of food,"

Mrs Peterson decided. "I'm sure there are some appetizers left."

Tristan opened his mouth as if he was about to start muttering about fishcakes again, but Andi silenced him with a fierce glance.

"Is it OK if we stay up here with Melissa?" Natalie asked. "The party's great, but Melissa needs us now."

"Of course," Mrs Peterson said, fanning herself vigorously. "But could you do me a favour first? Find your stepfather and get him to switch the air-conditioning on, even if that clacking noise is still there. Then try and get him downstairs or he'll miss the cake altogether!" She swept out of the room, shutting the door behind her.

"Tristan and I will look for Mr Peterson," Andi decided. "He said he was going to check the vents downstairs, didn't he?"

They found Mr Peterson and Mr Jacobs on their hands and knees in the downstairs bathroom, peering underneath the sink. They had taken the grille off the air-conditioning vent and Mr Jacobs was checking inside the flue. Andi cleared her throat and the two men looked up.

"Sorry to interrupt," she said, "but Mrs Peterson is looking for you, Mr Peterson. She'd like you to switch the air-conditioning on, even if it's still making a noise."

Mr Peterson climbed to his feet and dusted down his suit, which was looking even more crumpled than before. He picked up the plans of the house and studied them for a moment. "We've just got to check two more vents," he said. "One in the kitchen ceiling and one in the sun room."

"We found a loose-fitting valve in the study which could have been causing the noise," Mr Jacobs added. "I tightened it up, but we do need to check all the vents in the house before I can be sure that we've found the problem."

"Mrs Peterson wants to cut the cake in a few minutes," Tristan added meaningfully.

Mr Peterson held up his hands in defeat. "I get the message!" he said. "We'll check these last two, switch the system on, and then come in, I promise." He glanced at his watch. "It should only take ten minutes to look at these vents, so it'll be back on by eight o'clock."

Andi and Tristan checked on Jet and Buddy, who'd been shut in the dog room again. They were both panting with their mouths wide open when Andi and Tristan went in.

"Thank goodness Rascal never turned up in here," Andi said, scratching Buddy's tummy. "She would have got the fright of her life, meeting these two."

They fixed up a sign on the dog room door which read: THIS IS NOT A BATHROOM – DO NOT OPEN!, in case any more guests let the dogs out by mistake. Then, heading back to join Natalie and Melissa, they met Maria on the stairs. The housekeeper was balancing a tray containing four glasses of fizzy orange and four plates piled high with a selection of appetizers – including several fishcakes and a small pot of spicy dipping sauce.

Tristan's eyes lit up. "Fantastic," he murmured, taking the tray from Maria. "We'll take it from here, thanks."

"Maria?" Andi asked. "Could you please tell Mrs Peterson that the air-conditioning is going back on in ten minutes? Thanks!"

"Hurry up, Andi!" Tristan called over his shoulder as he carried the tray upstairs. "Or I'll eat your food as well!"

Soon they had laid out a feast on Natalie's bedroom carpet. Natalie switched off the main light and draped a set of fairy lights round the head of her bed. They helped create a party atmosphere as Andi, Tristan and Natalie took turns coaxing Melissa into eating something.

"Try the sticky rice balls," Natalie urged. "They're totally out of this world."

"I'm OK, thanks." Melissa gazed out of the window at the night sky and let out a heavy sigh.

"Let's get out our sleeping bags," Andi suggested, "and start this sleepover for real."

They laid the bags in a circle round the picnic rug. "It feels as if we're a group of cowboys in the desert," Tristan said, propping himself up on his elbow. He pretended to warm his hands over an imaginary campfire. "I was bo-orn," he began to sing in a tuneless voice, "under a wa-a-and'rin' star . . ."

"Shh!" Andi said. She prodded him so he fell over

on his side. "You'll annoy the rattlesnake I saw back there."

Tristan fanned himself with a folded napkin as the temperature in the bedroom grew hotter. Andi stretched across for a spring roll. She found she was on eye-level with the air-conditioning vent between Natalie's and Melissa's beds, and thought about how wonderful it would be to feel cool air coasting out of the vent and on to her face.

"Are Jet and Bud OK?" Natalie asked.

"Hot," Andi said. "I bet they can't wait for the air-conditioning to come on."

"They won't feel it in the dog room," Natalie said, reaching for another sticky rice ball. "There's no vent in there."

Andi dropped her spring roll.

"Don't you want that?" said Tristan hopefully.

Andi didn't reply. Instead, she scrambled to her feet and rushed over to the air vent. The grille was fixed to the wall on a hinge, so she could lift up the mesh with one finger and peer into the darkness.

"What on earth are you doing?" said Natalie.

"The air-conditioning," Andi muttered. "Why didn't we think of that before? There are vents everywhere in the house – you said so yourself, Nat. The grilles are on hinges! Could Rascal have pushed them open and got inside the system?"

The others stared at her, the food and drink forgotten. Even Melissa was looking up with hope flaring in her eyes.

"Are there vents in all the places where Rascal has been eating the food?" Andi prompted.

Natalie shook her head. "I don't know. But Geoff has got the plans. We could go and find out from him."

They ran downstairs to the kitchen. There was no sign of Mr Jacobs or Mr Peterson.

"Mr Peterson said there was a vent in the kitchen ceiling," Andi remembered, staring upward. "Remember how your mum found that nibbled plant on the shelf above the plate rack, Nat? That must have been how Rascal did it! She didn't jump up – she jumped *down*!"

"And then she must have jumped down to eat the

lettuce by the sink, and jumped across to the table to reach the apple," Natalie deduced, staring round the room, "and finally jumped to the floor." They all stared at a second vent set into the skirting board. It all made perfect sense.

Tristan pounced on a scroll of pale-blue paper lying on the table. "Here are the plans!"

Melissa grabbed the paper from him. "Kitchen, sun room, downstairs bathroom, study, games room," she said, tracing her finger across the plans. "There are vents in all those rooms!"

"Rascal must have been using the air-conditioning as tunnels," said Natalie, "just like a wild rabbit in a warren."

"And that's how she's moving from room to room without anyone seeing her!" Andi said in triumph.

Tristan raised his eyebrows. "Have we just solved another case?"

"Not yet," Andi warned. "But I think we're getting close."

Behind them, the kitchen clock chimed eight o'clock. Andi frowned. Someone had mentioned eight o'clock earlier, hadn't they?

"Oh no!" she gasped. "Mr Peterson is about to switch the system on!"

Melissa went white.

"Quick, Nat, where's the switch?" Andi said.

"In the garage."

"There's no time to lose," Andi said urgently. "We've got to stop them!"

They hurtled out of the kitchen and raced along the corridor. Mr Peterson and Mr Jacobs were standing together in the garage, Mr Jacobs cuddling Tiger and Mr Peterson's hand outstretched to flip the switch.

"Stop!" Andi yelled. *"Don't turn the air-conditioning on!"*

Looking astonished, Mr Peterson lowered his hand.

Natalie thrust the building plans under her stepfather's nose. "We think Rascal is inside the system!"

"Mr Jacobs, is it possible for a rabbit to travel through the air-conditioning?" Andi asked.

"Well, this is an old system," he said. "The pipes are pretty narrow. But yes – a rabbit could run around in there, if it was used to small spaces."

"Rascal loves her cardboard tunnels," Melissa explained. "The air-conditioning system must have seemed like a huge playground!"

Mrs Peterson rushed into the garage with several guests behind her. "I heard a scream! Is someone hurt?"

Andi quickly explained their theory.

"So Rascal really could be inside the air-conditioning?" Fisher said, stepping out from behind Nat's mum. "How are you going to get her out?"

"What about putting food next to each vent?" said Christine.

"What about using the dogs to flush her out?" Tristan suggested.

"Or Tiger?" Will offered.

"I wouldn't advise it," Fisher said, as Melissa looked alarmed. "We don't want to scare Rascal so much that she never comes out."

All the guests started talking, until Mr Peterson called for silence by waving his arms above his head. "Where's Melissa?"

Melissa put up her hand.

"Any tips on how to get Rascal out of the tunnels?" Mr Peterson asked.

"She usually comes when I rattle some food for her," Melissa said. "But now I've seen how complicated the air-conditioning system is, I think she must have been too far down a tunnel to hear me."

"I've got an idea," Andi announced. "There are more than a hundred guests here tonight, aren't there? How many vents are there in the house, Mr Peterson?"

"Sixteen," Mr Peterson said promptly.

"Could we put a couple of guests by each air vent?" Andi said. "They can listen for Rascal, and that way the whole house can be covered at the same time."

Mrs Peterson turned to her guests. "Would anyone object? As soon as we've found the rabbit, I promise we'll cut the cake."

"I'd be happy to help out," said the woman in the dark-blue dress who had mistakenly let the dogs out earlier.

Melissa and Natalie took charge of allotting a vent to each pair of guests, using the plans to make sure every vent was covered. Tristan asked the remaining guests to patrol the corridors between the rooms, in case Rascal made a break for it. Will took Mrs Greenstreet's arm to lead her to their vent, which was in the corridor leading to the garage.

Once everyone was in position, Melissa, Andi, Tristan and Natalie started moving steadily through the house. The Pet Finders kept very quiet, so the only sound was Melissa calling Rascal's name and rattling the bowl of food. Upstairs, the guests by each vent shook their heads, indicating they hadn't heard any sign of the rabbit in the vent. Downstairs bathroom, study, kitchen, sun room . . . still no trace of Rascal. Melissa bit her lip but kept going, although her voice was starting to tremble.

The last vent in the house was the one guarded by Will and Mrs Greenstreet. The old lady was standing very still with her head on one side. As Andi and the others approached, she held up her hand.

"Can you hear something?" Andi whispered.

Mrs Greenstreet nodded. "There!" she said suddenly, pointing at a section of the wall. "A scrabbling sound."

Andi listened, but she couldn't hear anything. Judging from the expressions on the faces of the others, neither could they.

"Um," Andi said, "are you sure?"

Mrs Greenstreet smiled as she ran her fingers lightly over the wall. "My hearing has become very finely tuned since I lost my sight," she said. "Your rabbit is moving that way." She pointed back towards the hall.

"I'll stay by the vent," Will offered. "You go with the others, Mrs Greenstreet. They need your ears."

Mrs Greenstreet nodded and took Andi's arm. Melissa ran down the passage, rattling the box.

"Scrabbling!" Tristan squeaked, pointing upwards. "I heard it! Rascal's headed upstairs!"

The guests by the downstairs vents started to appear in the hall when they heard the chase moving upstairs again. Mrs Greenstreet led the way with a confident tread: listening, listening . . .

As Andi grew used to the tiny, soft sounds of the rabbit hopping through the pipes, she found she could track Rascal's movements more easily. Judging from the sparkle in Melissa's eyes, so could she. Tristan and Natalie tracked Rascal's progress on the plans, moving their fingers along the mapped pipes and squabbling in hushed voices about which direction she was taking.

They followed Rascal along the landing towards one of the guest bedrooms. Andi ran ahead and held open the door so Melissa, Natalie, Tristan and Mrs Greenstreet could come in.

"The vent's under the window," Natalie whispered, looking up from the plans.

Melissa crouched down at the vent and rattled the food.

Come on, come on! Andi found herself willing the little rabbit along the pipes.

The scrabbling came closer and closer. Then, just inside the vent opening, it stopped.

Melissa took a handful of sunflower seeds out of the bowl and put them in a neat pile just outside the vent. Then she sat back to wait.

A woffly white nose peeped out. Rascal cautiously took a seed before backing into the pipe again. After a moment she came back for another. This time, she stayed at the entrance to the tunnel, munching her seed and looking round with bright black eyes. When she saw Melissa, she lifted her head and twitched her nose.

Very slowly, Melissa reached towards her, murmuring soothing nonsense the whole while. Andi was really impressed at her patience. Melissa's fingers moved closer and closer toward Rascal's fur, then gently smoothed her ears. Rascal tensed, but didn't try to run back into the tunnel. Melissa closed her hand firmly round the rabbit's tummy and lifted her up.

Andi shared a look of sheer triumph with Tristan. They'd done it! "You're so clever, finding all those lettuce leaves," Melissa whispered, kissing Rascal's head over and over. "I'm never going to lose you again, I promise."

The rabbit looked a little dusty, but her eyes were clear and she didn't look any the worse for her adventure in the walls.

"Amazing!" Tristan declared. "Mrs Greenstreet, MI5 could use your ears for spying. You were fantastic!"

"We should put Rascal back in her cage straight away," Natalie advised.

"And never let Maria vacuum the landing again," Andi joked.

Fisher and Will put their heads round the door. "Success?" Fisher asked.

"Success!" Andi announced with satisfaction.

"You Pet Finders have been incredible this week," Will said.

"Amazing, as Tristan would say," Mrs Greenstreet agreed, with a laugh.

There was a scrabbling at the door and Buddy put his nose inside the room. Melissa gasped and pulled Rascal tight against her.

"Looks as though one of the guests has opened the dog room door again," Andi sighed. "Come on, Bud. I know you're a Pet Finder, but this is one party you're not invited to!"

book 10

THE PET FINDERS CLUB

Help Honey!

Do you love animals?
Has your pet ever gone missing?

Well meet Andi, Tristan and Natalie —
The Pet Finders Club. Animals don't stay
lost for long with them hot on the trail!

A local pet show has got everyone excited,
and some people are being very competitive.
The Pet Finders are routing for Honey,
the beautiful Chihuahua to win but after
a chaotic afternoon at the grooming
parlour she's nowhere to be seen!

Will they find her in time for the show?